ARCHIE NOLAN

FAMILY
Detective

Published by
Donor Conception Network
154 Caledonian Road
London
N1 9RD
www.dcnetwork.org

Charity registration 1041297

© Donor Conception Network 2015

British Library Cataloguing in Publication Data
A catalogue record for this book is available from the British Library

ISBN 978-1-910222-22-5

Written by Beverley Ward
Illustrated by Spike Gerrell
Cover and book design by Andy Archer
Edited and project managed by Stephanie Clarkson

ARCHIE NOLAN

FAMILY
DETECTIVE

by BEVERLEY WARD
Illustrated by Spike Gerrell

www.dcnetwork.org

For Edie and Douglas.
B.W.

KeeP oUt !

PRivate !

Family Detectives

This ^diary belongs to:

Archie Nolan

Name: Archie Nolan

Age: 11

Birthday: February 11th

Star sign: Aquarius
(but astrology is just made-up, anyway.)

Address: 19 Bankhill Lane, Sheffield, England, UK, Earth, The Universe.

Best friends: Hamid Sadiq, Cameron Mellor.

Family: Mum, Dad, twin sister - Jemima, brother - Ryan.

Likes: Skateboarding, Doctor Who, Sherlock, CSI (don't tell Mum), comics, science.

Dislikes: Mark Doyle, the Family Detectives project, talking about feelings.

SUNDAY 2ND MARCH

So, this is me, Archie Nolan. I'm setting out on a voyage of self-discovery.

me ⟹

I'M tHe oNe FLYiNG tHe RocKeT!

That's what our teacher, Mrs Smithers, said when she introduced this stupid Family Detectives project at school. We've got to spend the term finding out all about our families and then tell everyone in the class what we've discovered.

When Mum heard about the project, she gave me this diary to write in because she thought it would help me to 'sort out my feelings' about being donor conceived. Not that I had any feelings that needed sorting out until Mrs Smithers decided to open up a whole can of worms.

Now my head feels like that can of worms and my thoughts are escaping all over the place, like this:

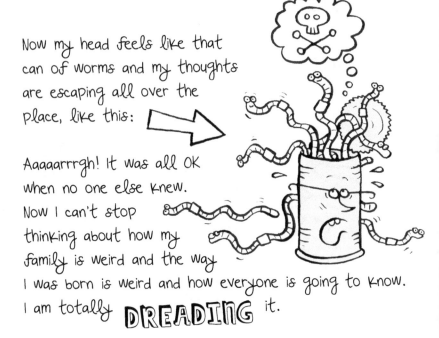

Aaaaarrrgh! It was all OK when no one else knew. Now I can't stop thinking about how my family is weird and the way I was born is weird and how everyone is going to know. I am totally **DREADING** it.

This is me on a good day, when I'm not having to talk about personal stuff that is

PRIVATE AND NONE OF ANYONE'S BUSINESS!!!!!

ME, ARCHIE ➡ NOLAN

I like drawing, but I mainly draw cartoons. I'm not so good at proper art. We did self-portraits in art class and Mark Doyle cracked up laughing at mine and said I looked like a total nerd. I tried to think of a clever reply, but four days later I still haven't come up with anything.

Mark had a point. It's pretty impossible to wear glasses and not look like a nerd and it's even harder to draw a cool portrait of yourself with specs.

When I said that to Hamid, he said that Arthur Crosby in our class looks good in specs.

⟵ Hamid

Then he pointed out that although she looks a lot like me, my twin sister Jemima isn't nerdy at all. "Jemima's portrait is amazing," he said. Hamid is my best friend, but you wouldn't know it sometimes.

Jemima →

annoying, ⟶ great at ART

Not a hair out of place

You'd think that the fact Jemima and me are twins would make us alike, but Mum says we're chalk and cheese. I'd say Jemima is the cheese. One of those posh French kinds that people eat with wine, a stinky one that oozes across the plate. And I'm skinny and pale, like chalk.

ME as CHaLK

HeR as CHeese

Actually, chalk and cheese aren't really that different if you analyse their properties. They're both white solids and they both contain calcium. The technical name for chalk is calcium carbonate and the chemical formula is $CaCO_3$. I know all that because I am **BRILLIANT** at science. Jemima might be amazing at art and English and be a prefect and on the school council and all that, but I came top in science last year and got picked for the National Science Fair.

When I grow up I'm going to be a forensic scientist like the ones on CSI. I've only seen it once, when I came downstairs because I couldn't sleep. I watched half an episode over Dad's shoulder before he noticed and sent me back to bed. It was really interesting. Then this guy from the police came into school last year and he said it would be a good career for someone like me who's observant and interested in science.

My dad works in a chemical laboratory making medicines so Mum says I take after him, which is odd because I don't actually have any of Dad's genes. Biologically speaking, I can't take after him. I don't have any of Mum's genes either. which is where this new school topic gets tricky.

MUM &
Dad

There's someone else in our house I'm nothing like - my brother Ryan. I may as well draw him, so if he picks this diary up he won't feel left out. Although I don't think he will pick the diary up because...

a) I'm planning on hiding it somewhere really safe.
b) Although he's 16, I'm not sure Ryan can read.

RYAN

Blimey, I've written loads. I'd better go now. Mum's shouting that dinner's on the table. We always have a Nolan family roast on a Sunday evening. The food's alright, but Mum and Dad like to have 'quality time' with us over dinner. GREAT!

MONDAY 3RD MARCH

School was OK today. We did cross-country trials. I came 6th. Hamid came second to last. He said he had a punctured lung, but Mr Jones the games teacher said it was just a stitch and made him go round again. Then Mrs Smithers talked about the Family Detectives project. She said it was going to be 'fabulous'. Mrs Smithers wears a lot of purple and thinks everything is fabulous. Don't get me wrong, she's nice, but she can be a bit much.

MRS SMITHERS

So anyway, Mrs Smithers said we are going to be finding out everything we can about our families and where we come from. All of which would be fine, except that while most people in my class were made from a little bit of their mum and a little bit of their dad, Jemima and I weren't made from Mum and Dad at all because we were donor conceived. This means that Mum and Dad are not our genetic parents. They used egg and sperm from donors to make us. Mum gave birth to us and they look after us and love us and tell us off just like every other mum and dad, but we don't get our DNA from them.

It's all pretty complicated! Luckily, because I love science I've learnt quite a bit about it.

Here's what I know...

We're all made up of genes and these genes are passed on from our genetic parents to us. It's important to be clear that genes is spelt with a 'g' and not a 'j'. Even if I could have my dad's jeans, I wouldn't want them because I'd look like this:

dad's JeaNS

I'd look even weirder in Mum's jeans!

This is what it says about genes in my 'WONDERS OF SCIENCE' book. My dad bought it for me and I've read it like, a million times.

MUM'S JEANS

Genes and DNA

Your body is made up of trillions of tiny units or cells.

Each cell has a control centre called a nucleus.

A Cell

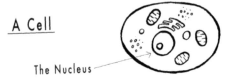

The Nucleus

Inside each nucleus a chemical called DNA forms long strands called chromosomes. A gene is a short section of DNA.

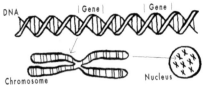

DNA | Gene | | Gene |

Chromosome   Nucleus

Almost all the body's cells have identical sets of genes stored in the nucleus. Genes carry the instructions for making your body and every person's genes are unique, except in the case of identical twins.

You get half your genes from your mother's egg and half from your father's sperm.

DID YOU KNOW?

1) Half of your genes are the same as a banana's!
2) There are about 25,000 genes inside a cell's nucleus.

34

I know some other stuff, too. Genes help to decide things about you like how tall you are and if you have blue eyes or brown eyes. My mum and dad both have perfect eyesight but, while Jemima's eyesight is fine, I'm shortsighted. Presumably one of our donors was shortsighted as well because that's another one of those things that's genetic.

You know that funny thing that some people can do where they roll their tongue up like a hot dog bun? Some people think that's down to genetics. I'm not convinced about that because I can do it really well, but when Jemima tries, her tongue looks more like a soggy lettuce leaf.

Genes don't just affect your body, they can affect your talents too. So, if you're really good at art or music or running, that might be because your genetic parents were really good at art or music or running. Of course you might be good at any of those things just because you have a gift, or you love them and practise really hard. Hamid and I practise skateboarding loads but he still spends most of his time falling off. Clearly good balance is not in his genes.

Genes can also affect your personality. So, if you're a bit of a worrier or annoyingly cheerful, you might have got that from one of your relatives, or it might be in your unique set of genes.

I wonder if Mrs Smithers' craziness is down to her inherited genes? If I had to guess where she came from, I'd say she was a cross between a Labrador puppy and a clown. But genetically-speaking that would be a disaster. And probably against the law.

THURSDAY 6TH MARCH

When I woke up this morning I just KNEW today was going to be a total nightmare. And guess what? I was right!

Last night's homework was to ask our parents about their families, ready for drawing our family tree. Mum and Dad had gone on their date night (bleurgh!) and we were left with Ryan. He was probably in his room, but there was no way I was going to knock and even if we did look in we would just see this:

Mum says Ryan's just going through an awkward teenage phase, but he seems to have been going through it for a very long time. When we were little he used to be quite fun. We used to play stuntmen on the trampoline. But that was before he turned all moody. Now he reckons trampolining is for losers.

So I phoned Hamid instead and told him how much I was dreading the project. He suggested that if I just pretended that I was made from a bit of Mum and a bit of Dad, like everyone else in the class, I could draw a simple family tree and the donor conception subject would be avoided completely.

It's not like everyone else's families are totally straightforward because quite a few kids have parents who are divorced and remarried and stuff. it's just that donor conception is on a whole different level. I know everyone's going to think it's weird and Mark Doyle's going to start picking on me again. I've only just recovered from the whole Christmas play disaster, which I'm really not going into.

donkey's Bottom

Anyway, I decided Ham's idea was a good one. Keep quiet and duck the whole topic. The only problem was that I forgot to discuss it with Jemima.

This afternoon in class, we were all sitting there ready to start drawing our family trees when Jemima 'Little Miss Keen' puts her hand up. I sat there silently clenching my fists, hoping she just needed the toilet but no, she came straight out with it, right there, in front of everyone.

"Mrs Smithers," she said, cool as a cucumber. "Do you want us to draw the family tree for the people in our <u>actual</u> families, or do you want us to draw our genetic family tree? It's a bit complicated for me and Archie because our parents used donor eggs and donor sperm to conceive us."

When she mentioned the word 'sperm' everyone started giggling. It felt like everyone was looking at me to see how I was going to react. So, of course, my face started burning and I basically turned into a tomato, which is probably one of those things that is genetic too. Thanks a lot, donor!

I was just sitting there imagining that my head was about to explode with embarrassment, splattering the room with tomato juice, when Mrs Smithers leaped up off her desk and flung her whiteboard marker across the room. She almost hit Jemima's best friend, Miriam, on the head.

"Oh! This is fascinating," she said. "You must tell us all about it. This will add such an interesting dimension to our Family Detectives project."

I gave Jemima a 'thanks for that' glare and accidentally looked straight at Mark Doyle. Big mistake. It's never a good idea to look him in the eye unless you want to spend your break time in a headlock. He had a horrible smirk on his face and he mouthed something. Mrs Smithers didn't see or hear him, but I did. He said,

"**FREAK!**"

So now it's out there. And Mark Doyle (and probably everyone else in the class) thinks I'm a freak. I almost wish I could go back to being the speccy science nerd who had to dress up as the back end of the donkey in the school play. Doh! I said I wasn't going to talk about that.

So yeah. Today was a nightmare. I'm just going to stop writing and go to sleep to put an end to it right now. As Mum always says, 'Tomorrow's another day...' And hey, things can't possibly get worse, can they?

SUNDAY 9TH MARCH

Yesterday we went out to the countryside to see Cameron. Cam is my other best friend, but he doesn't live that near us and he goes to a different school. He's donor conceived like me and Jemima, but his mum, Hazel, had him on her own.

CAM ⟹

Knowing Mum, she probably phoned Hazel and suggested an urgent meeting of the SDDCC now that she knows we've been outed at school.

The SDDCC stands for The Sheffield and Derbyshire Donor Conception Club which is a ridiculously long name for a club made up of just three members - me, Jemima and Cameron. Cam is the only donor conceived child that me and Jemima know. Cam used to hang out with a few other kids with solo mums because his mum was part of this group that met when he was a baby. He said that was good because when he started school he found it really hard with people asking about his dad all the time. He says that those kids understood. He doesn't see so much of them now he's older though.

Mum and Hazel met at some kind of donor conception workshop in Nottingham when they were both pregnant. They're what they like to call 'loud and proud' about the whole donor thing and they're always going off to events. Recently mum's been going on at me about this conference for donor conception families. She and Dad want to take Jemima and me.

NEWSFLASH!
NOT GONNA HAPPEN!

Anyway, although originally we only met cause our mums were friends, luckily Cam is really cool to hang out with, so we see him a lot. Because it's just Cam and his mum in their house they really like having people over and his mum always makes amazing teas with brilliant cakes.

YUM!! ⟵ YUM!!

The SDDCC usually meets in the tree house at the bottom of Cameron's garden.

where he lives is amazing. His house is built into the hillside just under a ledge that's famous with rock climbers. when you're in the tree house, you can see for miles.

It's a bit of a squeeze now we're older but it's a pretty cool place to be, especially when you want to discuss stuff in private. Like yesterday.

I was telling Cameron all about the nightmare Family Detectives project when Jemima butted in and said we should be proud to be donor conceived cause it makes us 'special'.

Cameron and I looked at each other and rolled our eyes. Jemima's always saying stuff like that.

Cam said he didn't like being special. He reckons being the only kid in school without a dad and having the only single mum in the village sucks.

That set Jemima off. She told him he was bonkers and that he should be proud to be special with his garden that is like an outdoor activity centre and his amazing mum who's an entrepreneur with her own business.

Then Cameron started on about how his mum should have chosen a donor who looked like her. Cam's mum has pale skin, blonde hair and green eyes but she chose a donor of Hispanic origin from California. Apparently he was very clever and he sounded really kind and interesting in his profile, which is why Cam's mum chose him.

If you saw Cameron, you'd totally think he was Spanish or something. He has dark, wavy hair and brown eyes and looks nothing like his mum at all.

"And I don't have any brothers and sisters," Cam said. He was sounding a bit moany now to be honest and for once I agreed with Jemima when she said that brothers and sisters aren't all they're cracked up to be.

"Have you met Ryan?" she said.

That shut Cam up. The last time Cam came round Ryan squashed us under the sofa cushions and farted on our heads.

After lunch Jemima went off for a walk with Hazel and Mum. Cam and I went looking round the outdoor shops. Sometimes when we go out to the countryside we go climbing on the rocks above Cam's place, but by the afternoon it was chucking it down.

We were in Moorlands Outdoor Store looking at the camping stuff when we spotted him. There was a man standing just across the aisle from us, looking at the rucksacks and holdalls. He was about Gramps' age but he wasn't dressed like Gramps. He didn't fit in with all the outdoorsy types in their hiking boots and fleeces either. He was wearing a long black coat and leather gloves even though it wasn't really that cold. His skin was pale, almost ghostly white and he had dark bags under his eyes. What was left of his grey hair was scraped back from his forehead.

I pointed him out to Cameron. Well, I didn't point. I used our secret code language, which is basically putting the word 'egg' before every vowel. I found the code on the Internet. It's hard to pick up, but once you can say it really fast it sounds like crazy talk to anyone else..

So I said...

"cheggeck eggout thegge weggeird eggold gegguy."

But what I was ACTUALLY saying was...

"Check out the weird old guy."

Cam code-replied that the man runs the village grocery store with his wife. Apparently he's always staring at Cam.

Cue the usual jokes about Cam's 'beautiful hair' from me. Whenever we go round the shops in the village all the old ladies go on about his lovely hair.

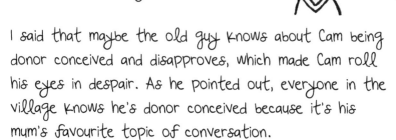

I said that maybe the old guy knows about Cam being donor conceived and disapproves, which made Cam roll his eyes in despair. As he pointed out, everyone in the village knows he's donor conceived because it's his mum's favourite topic of conversation.

I pretended to look at the screw top on a flask, but really I was staring at the man again, trying to work him out. He definitely looked shifty. Suddenly he turned his head and stared at me. I swear it felt like I'd been shoved inside a freezer. He had these piercing eyes. Ice blue. Cold! The hairs on the back of my neck stood up.

I looked at Cameron. He was standing like a statue, frozen by the man's evil death-glare. I think he would still be there now if I hadn't grabbed his arm and dragged him out of the shop.

DEATH ⇨⇨⇨⇨ GLARE!!

We were so spooked we ran up the road and hid round the side of the fish and chip shop. A little while later, the old guy walked past, on his way back to his grocery store. Cam said his name is Mr Marsden. Mr Martian more like! There's something not right about that man.

His shop is weird, too. The window has the usual kind of stuff in it - boxes of fruit, vegetables and packets of pasta and stuff - but in between there are weird things, like a Halloween lantern even though it's nearly Easter, a spooky-looking gnome holding a bunch of flowers, and a portrait of Prince Charles and Princess Diana, who died about twenty years ago. There's definitely something fishy going on. Cam and I have decided to find out what it is.

One thing's for sure, investigating Mr Marsden is DEFINITELY more interesting than drawing a diagram of my messed up family.

TUESDAY 11TH MARCH

I was supposed to hand my family tree in today. I had a go at drawing it last night, but there were so many people and branches that it came out looking like a tarantula had fallen in a pot of ink and then run about on my paper.

When I'd finished, my family tree looked like this:

I sneaked a look at Jemima's.

It looked like this:

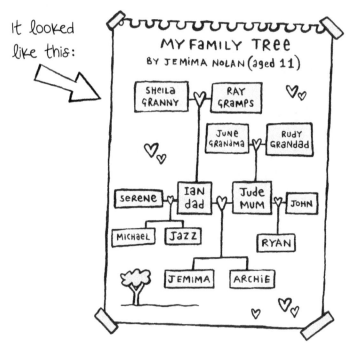

In the end I left mine at home.

Maybe I would have got away with it, but Jemima's friend, Miriam, is homework monitor so she just loved shouting, "Archie Nolan hasn't handed his family tree in, Miss!" And then I got called up to Mrs Smithers' desk for 'a little chat' while everyone else went home. She wanted to know if I'd forgotten my homework or not done it at all and when I said I hadn't finished it because it was a big mess, she asked me if everything was all right. I just looked at the floor.

She put her hand on my shoulder and for one amazing minute I thought she was going to let me off the project but... no. She said not to worry about the drawing, and, if I felt funny about standing up and talking through my family tree, to try writing it all down instead. At least it looks like I won't have to do a presentation. Result!!!!

THURSDAY 13TH MARCH

So, I'm going to try writing about my family in here first. That way I can double-check the weirdness factor before I put it in my special folder.

My family starts out in a fairly straightforward way. I've only gone as far back as my grandparents because, to be honest, trying to explain even three generations of my family is complicated enough.

My Gramps (Ray) met Granny (Sheila) in Leeds and they got married and had my dad, Ian, in the fifties. I don't know much about how Gramps and Granny met because Granny died a few years ago and as

Gramps says, he's "not one for talking."

Meanwhile, a bit later my other Grandad (Rudy) met my Grandma (June) over here in Sheffield. Apparently he met her at a dance. Mum tells me that Grandad used to say that she could do the twist like no other girl in town. I've no idea what he means and it sounds like the kind of thing it's best <u>not</u> to know. Anyway, they got married and had my mum and they called her Judy because it was a mix of their names. Jemima thinks it's cute. I think it's a bit lame - like they couldn't be bothered to even look at any baby name books. Mum always calls herself Jude so I think she probably agrees with me.

So far, so normal - but now it starts to get messy.

Dad grew up and came to Sheffield University to study chemistry and according to Gramps,

"That's not all he were studying!" He's talking about Dad's first marriage to Serene.

SERENE

Before they "made each other miserable", Dad and Serene got married and had two children, Jazz (short for Jasmine) and Michael. They are kind of my half-sister and brother - except I'm not sure if they are because with me being donor conceived, we're not actually genetically related. Plus they were born way before we were in the seventies, so they're ancient, old enough to be my parents really.

JAZZ   MICHAEL

Jazz and Michael were conceived 'the usual way', so their mum and dad (Serene and my dad) are their biological parents. They also brought them up.

And then Dad and Serene decided that they didn't want any more children. I don't know why. Dad had an operation, I think it's called a vasectomy, which meant that he couldn't have any more kids. If he hadn't done that maybe Jemima and I would still have been able to be made with a bit of Dad's genes. But then I guess we wouldn't really be me and Jemima, we'd be two different people.

So while Dad was having kids with Serene, Mum trained as a teacher and lived all over the world. While she was in America she met a guy called John. In our house, John is usually known as 'Hippy John', even when Ryan is around.

I've only met John a few times because he's abroad a lot but I like to think they call him a hippy because his trousers are always hanging off his hips.

HiPPY JOHN ⟹

Apparently Mum and John were dating for a bit but he kept going off round the world and they weren't exactly planning Ryan. So Ryan also wasn't conceived with the help of a donor. That means that Mum and Hippy John are Ryan's biological parents. John isn't around much though, so to be honest, he isn't really like a proper dad to Ryan.

Mum says Ryan is a lovely boy, really. Well Ryan may have been cute when he was little, but looking at him now I'm not sure 'lovely' is the word I'd use to describe my brother. 'Angry'? Sure. 'Rude'? Definitely. But 'lovely'? Nah.

Anyway, Mum and Hippy John had Ryan, but then Hippy John decided that he wanted to go off round Africa in a camper van even though they'd just had baby Ryan. Mum and Dad get very cross about John's behaviour but if Ryan were my son, I might consider driving to Timbuktu.

Around the same time, Serene fell in love with her personal trainer. So Dad got divorced, Hippy John went off travelling and Mum and Dad were both on their own for a while feeling sad.

And then things got better. Mum moved back to Sheffield and went to work in the office at the laboratory where Dad mixes chemicals to make medicines. They met at the office Christmas party in 1999 and apparently it was 'love at first sight' and 'true love second time around' and all kinds of soppy stuff like that. They got married in 2001 and Gramps got drunk and made a toast and called Mum 'Serene' by accident.

Then it gets even more complicated because Mum and Dad wanted children together, but they couldn't because of Dad's vasectomy operation. They went to a clinic and tried to use a sperm donor to solve the problem. But it turned out that as Mum was getting older her eggs were out of date or something. So for a while they were just really sad and didn't know what to do next. Then the clinic suggested that they could use an egg donor as well as a sperm donor. So, they went ahead and - Ta Dah! - they got me and Jemima.

BARGAIN
2 for the price of 1

Dad always says it was 'Buy One Get One Free' at the clinic. I'm the eldest by ten minutes so I like to think that I'm the real deal and Jemima is the free extra. She disagrees.

Oh and there's one more thing. Jazz is now married to Martha. They are lesbians. Because they're both women and only have eggs and no sperm, they asked their friend Jake - who is also gay - to give them some sperm, so they could have a baby. I don't know if they used Jazz or Martha's egg, but anyway, the egg and Jake's sperm turned into my niece Ella - who is the same age as me and Jemima. Weird, or what?

And that's my family tree! Complicated. Embarrassing. Weird. Take your pick.

FRIDAY 14TH MARCH

Well. Another great day - not! After all that effort getting my family tree writing done last night, Mrs. Smithers didn't even ask for it. She was too busy getting excited about the Easter Assembly. You should have seen Mark Doyle's face when Mrs. Smithers delved into the props box and said, "I've got a lovely pair of bunny ears and the sweetest fluffy tail for you, Archie."

I'm so angry, I've been playing Astro Blast in my room all evening, which has made me feel a bit better. Chatting to Cam on Skype cheered me up, too. Today he saw that old guy, Mr Marsden, in the graveyard in Hathersage. I didn't have to ask what Cam was doing in the graveyard because I already know. He'll have been doing what he's always doing. Climbing something. That's not what Mr Marsden was up to though. Apparently he was just hanging around eating sandwiches.

Cam thinks he must be a vampire. I'd almost agree with him, if it weren't for the following...

YUK

a) Vampires don't go outside in daylight.
b) Vampires tend to prefer sucking blood to munching on cheese butties.
c) Everyone knows VAMPIRES DON'T EXIST. (Everyone except for Jemima of course.)

Jemima's obsessed with that book 'Twilight' and when I told her about Mr Marsden she was totally convinced about the vampire theory. She said she'd seen him in the graveyard too, when she was sketching in the church for her art project. Which I admit, is more than a bit odd.

Anyway, the great news is, Cam has invited me for a sleepover during the Easter holidays so we can do some proper investigating. Now I just have to convince Mum.

WEDNESDAY 19TH MARCH

Well after today my life is over! You might as well put me in a graveyard with 'Vampire' Marsden and let him do his worst.

We did the lesson hearing about everyone's families. It wasn't too bad at first. I thought I knew most things about the people in my class but it turns out lots of them have weird relatives or strange setups. None of them as weird as ours of course, but it did make me feel a bit better about our crazy family.

For instance, for ten years Miriam thought her auntie Sheila was her mum and her mum was her auntie. I don't know how they got that mixed up! Families are strange.

When Hamid presented his family story, I realised I didn't know much about him at all. Which is pretty rubbish for a best friend. There are always a lot of people hanging around when you go to Hamid's house for tea, but I didn't know that his Uncle Fiaz and Aunt Jamila live with him. Or that Uncle Fiaz and Aunt Jamila are actually his second cousins once removed. How could I not know that? I've been round there eating samosas since I was about seven.

Jacob Taylor's grandad used to play football for Manchester United, which seriously makes you wonder about Jacob's genetic

tasty SAMOSAS

makeup because he's the worst footballer I've ever seen. He's even worse than Hamid and that's saying something. He's always stuck in goal even though he's tiny and skinny. I think the footie lads do it to him just so they have someone to blame when they lose because Jacob Taylor can't catch to save his life.

Abusammed didn't say much as usual, but Mrs Smithers told us that his dad was some kind of war hero in Somalia. Abusammed smiled when she said that. He's only been in our class for a few months and he lives with his aunt and uncle now. I knew he was a refugee, but never really thought about what that means before. Turns out he's a refugee and an orphan. I'm going to try to remember that next time he flicks chewed-up paper at my head during English. If I was a refugee orphan, maybe I'd do annoying stuff, too.

When it got to me Mrs Smithers just collected my book, then she asked Jemima to present her family tree to the class. I thought I was off the hook. Then right at the last minute, she suggested that I might like to stand up next to Jemima. My cunning plan had completely failed! I ended up in front of the class looking like a right lemon.

A Right LEMON

Jemima loves being the centre of attention. When I say that I don't just mean that she likes to sit at the head of the table for dinner (though she does) or that she likes to talk a lot (which she also does, on and on and on). No, Jemima is the kind of irritating kid who always has her hand up to answer questions in class and the person who leaps up to volunteer for jobs.

So standing up and talking about our weird and wonderful family is her idea of heaven. Standing next to her while she does this is my idea of **HELL**.

Me Me Me Me

She started by explaining all about eggs and sperm and about how Mum and Dad couldn't conceive us on their own, then she moved on to talking about donors. She'd obviously done her research because she was telling the whole class things that even I didn't know. It's not surprising really because she's always asking questions and I don't usually listen when Mum and Dad talk about this stuff, but I was starting to wish I'd paid more attention.

Jemima told the class that our male donor was six foot two and that both donors had blonde hair and blue eyes, like me and Jemima. While she was saying this she pointed towards me as if I was the evidence in a courtroom drama.

I looked round and everyone seemed pretty interested. I was beginning to think that maybe it would all be ok and then...

My annoying sister dropped a massive bomb on me.

She said that donors in the UK are allowed to donate sperm to up to ten families. That means we might have ten or more half-brothers and half-sisters and that, even worse, there might actually be other children with some of our genetic make-up in our school.

Aaaargh! How has no one ever told me this before? I looked round the class, searching for signs of anyone who looks like me. Everyone was looking totally freaked out. I don't blame them. I felt totally sick inside. Jemima was still talking. She'd gone on to egg donation and was saying how eggs are really tiny and so getting them out of the woman's body is tricky and that some women donate eggs when they're having IVF treatment to try to have their own babies.

Mrs Smithers was nodding, but I just kept looking at the rest of the class to see if anyone looked like me. Some of them were whispering and giggling and when I stared at Arthur Crosby, I swear his face started morphing into mine.

What if we are related? He has glasses like me, blonde hair, blue eyes. I could feel my skin starting to sweat and, for a moment, I thought I really was going to be sick.

ARTHUR

And then Mark Doyle put his hand up. Everyone stared. Mark Doyle NEVER puts his hand up in class.

Mrs Smithers was obviously thinking what I was thinking because she asked him if he needed the loo, but instead he started saying about how he was conceived by IVF! I couldn't believe it. When he talked about it his face went all soft, like dough all of a sudden, and I pictured his mum and dad holding the baby they'd wanted so much. Mum's friend, Melissa, had IVF and I've heard her and Mum comparing notes about how complicated it is because Mum had to use IVF to have us. They're always going on about how precious IVF babies are and stuff.

I sat there imagining Mark Doyle as a baby. It was like I was hallucinating. Maybe it was the smell of the whiteboard marker that Jemima had been waving about in my face?

Obviously, Mrs Smithers thought Mark Doyle's IVF conception was fantastic. And then she dismissed us for lunch and told us to go straight to the dining room.

Instead, I went straight to the toilet, locked myself in a cubicle, stuffed the ends of my jumper sleeves in my mouth, and screamed.

When I finally came out, Hamid was waiting. He said he didn't think the presentation had gone too badly. He said it was "interesting" to hear about how I might have hundreds of brothers and sisters. Then, to make matters worse, he started discussing percentages and the probability of there being a pair of twins just like me and Jemima in the same city.

Hamid is brilliant at maths, but he really does not have a clue when to shut up.

THURSDAY 20TH MARCH

I was still annoyed with Hamid when I got to school today so I went off and played football at first break to avoid him. But then he came up to me in the lunch queue. He said he thought my donor story was cool. I told him I didn't want to talk about it any more.

I know I was sounding really angry and it wasn't Ham's fault, but I really felt like punching someone. And there was Daniel Saunders as soon as I collected my tray, waving a hard-boiled egg under Jemima's nose. It's a good job that he's no match for my sister, otherwise I really might have hit him.

"Look what I've got for lunch," he said. "Eggs! Have you got any sperm? We could make a baby."

Daniel's friends cracked up laughing, although I noticed Mark Doyle just stared into his lunchbox.

Sometimes I'm really proud of my sister. She was awesome. She put down her tray and turned on Daniel. "Firstly," she said, "that's a hen's egg and not a human egg. And secondly, it's hard-boiled so not able to be fertilised."

SCARY FIERCE

Daniel looked as if he'd just scored an own goal. Then he spotted me.

"Hey, Nolan," he shouted loudly so that the girls on the next table could hear. "We know where you come from!"

I knew what he was after, but I wasn't going to give him the satisfaction. For once I'd thought of something funny to say right there on the spot.

"Where?" I asked. "Sheffield?"

Ha! Get in! Back of the net!

The girls thought it was funny, too. But Daniel was really mad. He said "Did you get your sense of humour from your doughnut dad?"

He fell right into it. Half the dining room was laughing before I had even said anything.

"Doughnut?" I laughed - "It's DONOR, you numpty. Where did you get your brains from? Poundland?"

I don't know why I said Poundland but it shut Daniel right up. Hamid and I walked up to the hatch to get our lunch. Egg, chips and salad!

And it was doughnuts for pudding. Ha! My favourite.

JAM   CHOCOLATE   SPRINKLES

Contrary to what 'Dozy Danny' Saunders thinks, donors have nothing whatsoever to do with doughnuts.

This is what it says in my dictionary about doughnuts...

> **doughnut** or **donut** (US) *noun*
> A small fried cake of sweetened dough, typically in the shape of a ball or ring.

This is what it says in my dictionary about donors...

> **donor** *noun*
> A giver; a person who provides blood, tissue, sperm, eggs, embryos or organs for transplant in others.

Maybe I should pinch Daniel Saunders' jotter out of his tray tomorrow and draw him a diagram so he can see that the two are very different.

A DOUGHNUT

A DONOR

Donors donate eggs, sperm or embryos to be used by people who can't have babies without help. Mum says there are lots of reasons why people can't always make their own babies. She was already forty-two when she married my dad and that's quite late for a woman to start trying for a baby. She says it's "a cruel quirk of nature" that women are supposed to have children when they're in their twenties and thirties when they're not always very good at choosing the right partners. (I reckon she's talking about Hippy John.)

Some women can't make their own babies because they've had cancer or maybe just because they were born with some other medical problem.

It's the same with men. Some men don't make enough sperm or the right kind of sperm or sometimes their sperm just doesn't work properly. Or, like my dad, they might have had a vasectomy which stops them from being able to make babies.

That's for the couples where you've got a man and a woman. But a single woman or man might need a donor because they haven't met someone to have kids with.

And then a lesbian or gay couple would also need a donor because two eggs or two sperm won't add up to a baby. You need one of each!

Mum said sometimes a woman can't carry the baby in her womb because of medical problems and then she would have to ask another woman, who is called a surrogate, to carry the baby for her.

My head hurt when Mum went through all these possibilities. I got really confused so I asked her to write it down to help me understand it better and it must have helped cause I've just explained it all again.

So, donors are really generous and important people because they give a part of themselves to help others who really want to be parents. Without them, Jemima and I wouldn't exist and Mum and Dad would have been sad forever.

P.S. Doughnuts are also really nice.

SATURDAY 22ND MARCH

Mum noticed that I was a bit quiet today. Since the awful Family Detectives day on Wednesday, I've mostly been shooting stuff on my DS. It doesn't matter what I shoot, it's just the action of shooting things and watching them break apart that makes me feel better. It must be getting out of hand though because in my dream last night I found myself shooting little donor eggs with faces that looked like me and Jemima.

Mum asked me if I wanted to help her to wash the car, which was just a ploy to get me to talk, but I didn't mind. As soon as we got outside she threw the soapy sponge at me.

Mum's like that when she's in a good mood. She's pretty fun really. When you go round to some friends' houses, their mums are all serious and you feel scared that you might do the wrong thing by not taking your shoes off or forgetting to say thank you. My mum's not like that. Friends really like coming round to our place.

I started soaping the car with the sponge. The warm water was kind of soothing on my hands and I liked watching the white foam cover up the dirt. She asked me how the project was going. I told her it was fine. I don't know why people say 'fine' because they never mean it. I certainly didn't.

Then she started asking me how it had been for me standing next to Jemima while she told the whole class about eggs and sperm and about our personal family stuff. Well, that's not exactly what she said. I told her it was probably my best day ever. NOT! She came and sat down where I was cleaning the hubcaps.

That was the last thing I needed. I tried to do that thing where you squeeze your eyes shut to stop yourself from crying, but then the stupid things dripped out instead of going back in. I turned my head away and was going to leave it there, but then I thought I may as well seize the moment and ask her if it was true, this thing about there being genetic half brothers and sisters all over the place.

Mum put her arm round me. She still had the sponge in her hand and the water was soaking into my hoody and she told me that it is true. Then she tried to make out like it's not that big of a deal.

I couldn't help it. I kind of lost it then and started shouting about how freaked out I was and how there might be hundreds of people with my genes wandering around Sheffield.

AAAAAAAAAAAAARRRRGHHHHH!!!!!

Mum said there wouldn't be hundreds, maybe just a few, and none exactly like me and Jemima. I'm not convinced! A few is still a few. Arthur Crosby could still be my genetic half brother. And how would I know?

And then - and this 'takes the barm cake' as Gramps would say - according to Mum, I may never know. Even if she asked the clinic they could only tell her how many half brothers and sisters I've got. She called them half siblings - which I prefer because I don't want to use the word 'brother' or 'sister' for someone I've never met. Anyway, Mum said they wouldn't tell me their names or anything. She said I might be able to get in touch with them when I'm eighteen though, maybe, via this thing called Donor Sibling Link. I've no idea if I'd want to. It's all too weird.

Mum said I don't have to ever meet any of them if I don't want to and frankly, that sounds best to me. The less donor conceived people I have to meet the better. Which is why I have absolutely no intention of going to the conference she keeps mentioning.

She started on about it again then. She said I should give it some serious thought, because she thinks I'll find it interesting. Interesting? Meeting loads of donor conceived strangers? I don't think so. I shook my head so hard I thought it might fall off. No way was I going to sit in a room full of other 'freaks' talking about feelings.

When Mum realised the subject was closed she went all soppy, talking about how what matters is the people around you who love you and that if we go back a few generations we might all be related to lots of people we don't know. And then she pulled her trump card by saying how lucky I am to have Jemima who is my biological twin that I get to grow up with and hang around with for the rest of my life, as if that's supposed to cheer me up.

Mum gave me a squeeze and the water started to seep right through to my skin. I couldn't wait to get inside but when I asked her if she was done soaking me she lifted the sponge up and squeezed it right over my head so that the water was running down my face.

Still, at least Ryan and Jemima couldn't see I'd been crying.

MONDAY 24TH MARCH

I've just finished Skyping with Cameron. We compared notes about some of the daft stuff that people at school say about being DC which made me feel a bit better. It sounds like people in his school are even more idiotic than the kids in mine (and that's saying something). One girl in Cam's class even asked him if he was an alien.

And he's had all these people ask him where his dad is. He's told me this before. It doesn't matter how many times Cam tells people that he doesn't have a dad, they just don't get it. They think his parents must be divorced or his dad must be dead or he must be an orphan. They don't get that sperm + egg = baby, but dads don't necessarily come into it.

Anyway, the most interesting thing he told me was about that vampire dude, Mr Marsden. Cameron's been watching him and apparently, every time his wife leaves the shop he turns the sign on the door to 'CLOSED', but doesn't come out. Seriously suspicious. What's he doing in there that he doesn't want her to know about?

I can find out when I go over there for a sleepover in a week or two. Cam's mum has told him Mr Marsden's just a harmless old man with dodgy fashion sense, but with the death-stare, the graveyard and now the shop closing, we know different.

TUESDAY 25TH MARCH

Word has obviously got back to Mrs S that the whole donor conception thing has been causing some excitement around the school because today she asked Jemima and me if we would mind answering some questions about being donor conceived.

Mrs Smithers has this way about her that means that even when you don't want to do something you do it anyway. And let me tell you, I REALLY didn't want to do this. We had to go and stand back up in front of the class while Mrs Smithers perched on her desk.

"Who's got a question for Archie and Jemima?" she asked. "Fire away!" Ha! Good choice of words. Standing there felt just like being in front of a firing squad.

Here's just some of what we got asked... and what Jemima replied. (For once I agreed with absolutely everything that came out of her mouth.)

64

At this point Millie Jones said she still didn't get it. As Gramps would say, "The lights are on but there's no-one home." So for Millie Jones and everyone else's sake Jemima drew a diagram, which looked like this:

But the questions kept coming and in the end I had to get involved because people are so clueless.

"So it's like being adopted?"

"No. Only in that we're not genetically related to our parents. But Mum and Dad planned us from day one and Mum carried us and gave birth to us. They just made us from other people's eggs and sperm."

"Would you like to see your real mum and dad?"

"We do see our real mum and dad. We see them in the morning and after school and pretty much every day. Our real mum and dad are the people who look after

us. The others just provided a bit of genetic material.
It might be important but, that doesn't make you a parent."

"Will you ever be able to meet your donors?"

"Probably not. The law changed in 2005. If you were
conceived before 2005 like us, you don't have any right
to meet your donor, unless they re-register later
to say they're happy to be identifiable. If you were
donor conceived after 2005 here in the UK, you have the
right to contact your donor once you turn eighteen if
you want to, because nowadays donors have to sign
something to say they don't mind being put in touch
with the families they help."

"What about your half-siblings?"

"We could meet them. Anyone born since 1991 can put
their names on the Donor Sibling Link once they're
eighteen to have contact with half siblings - if
both sides agree."

"What do you know about your donors?"
(That was Hamid. Why did he have to prolong my agony?)

"Not much, just things like their height and hair colour.
Mum says it depends where you get the donation from."

If you go abroad, some clinics can give you loads of information about the donor. Others hardly give anything at all. You never get to know the donor's name unless you actually already know the donor- like if they're your next door neighbour or something. In this country, you get a bit of information, but not that much. which is fine by me."

Finally, they ran out of questions - but only just before last bell. 'Surely that has to be it?' I was thinking. 'I mean, what on earth else could everyone possibly want to know about me?' Even I've learnt stuff I didn't know about donor conception. But no. Mrs Smithers now says we've got to interview our family members over Easter so we can make a map of our families next term. ...Fabulous!

WEDNESDAY 26TH MARCH

After school today I went to Hamid's for a bit. Because he's the oldest, sometimes Hamid has to bring his sister and his cousin home from school with him. His sister, Shobna, is in Year 4 and his cousin, Zaffar is still in Infants. We picked them up and walked up the hill past my house and over to Hamid's.

ZaffaR → shobNa ↓ HaMid's dad → Hamid ↓ HaMid's MuM & the BaBy ↓

Hamid's mum was home and feeding the baby when we got there. Ham has taught me to say 'as-salamu alaykum', but I feel a bit silly saying it to his mum. So I just said, "Hello" and dived into the Pakistani sweets she always has out. We were about to go up to Ham's room but Ham had obviously been talking to her about the school project because then Mrs Sadiq started asking questions about donor conception. She wanted to know whether it might be good for her cousin in Australia who has been trying for a baby for about five years and has had IVF which didn't work. "My cousin might need a bit more help than usual," she told me. I nodded politely, but <u>really</u>? TMI!! (Too Much Information!) Just because I'm donor conceived, it doesn't mean I'm an expert on the subject.

Next thing she was asking Hamid if he thought that little Zaynab down the road might be donor conceived because she didn't look anything like her parents.

"I bet there's more of it about than we know. What do you think Archie?"

I just nodded some more and shoved another sweet into my mouth.

IS NOWHERE A DONOR CONCEPTION-FREE ZONE?

THURSDAY 27TH MARCH

Guess what? Today's Family Detectives lesson actually wasn't that bad. **SHOCK HORROR!**

Mrs Smithers had got hold of some recording equipment and we learned how to do interviews like real detectives do.

me as an
**ace
detective**
⟹

I spent most of the lesson interviewing Arthur Crosby, which turned out to be a bit of a relief because I couldn't find any holes in his story about his family. It really sounds like he wasn't donor conceived at all, so I think I can relax about him being my half brother.

Next we had to make what Mrs Smithers called 'a transcript' of the interview. We had to write down all the questions and all the answers exactly as it was recorded. She said people do this in courtrooms and stuff to make sure that all the facts are there as evidence. It was weird writing it all down, because when you write how people talk it sounds a bit odd. People say, 'um' and 'er' and pause in funny places and start again.

Anyway. It turns out Dad has a little voice recorder at home and he's going to let me and Jemima borrow it to do our family interviews and then I'm going to write up the transcripts in my diary. I think it'll be good practice for if I become a detective. The deeper I get involved with the Mr Marsden case, the more I think I might like to be a detective and not just do the forensic stuff.

So tonight I borrowed Dad's voice recorder and interviewed Ryan. And this is what I got.

Interview commenced: 19:00
Thursday 27th March

"So, first of all, for the readers, could you just tell me your name and your age?"

"What?"

"Your name?"

"What for? You know my name."

"It's just a formality. Just a good way to start."

"No it's not. It's a stupid way to start."

"Ok. So, you and me live in the same house and we're brought up by the same parents even though, technically, we're not genetically related. What's that like?"

"What do you mean, what's that like? What do you think it's like?"

"I don't know. That's why I'm asking you."

"It sucks. Like everything about this family."

"Moving on... What do you think about the fact that Jemima and I are donor conceived? Do you still think of us as your brother and sister even though we're not genetically related?"

"I don't know. What does it matter? You'd still be just as annoying even if we were genetically related."

"Thanks. The feeling's mutual. What about Dad? You kind of have two dads. Hippy John is your biological father, but Dad brought you up, didn't he?"

"You could say that, I suppose, if you think that playing naff jazz music at a person is bringing them up."

"Fair point. John does have better taste in music."

"Yeah. Like that makes him a great father. Loser."

"Do you think your family has anything to do with your anger issues?"

"What anger issues? I don't have anger issues, you idiot. You say that again and I'll kill you."

Interview terminated at 19:08 due to threats of violence.

SATURDAY 29TH MARCH

I'm in Cam's tree house writing this. It's late and Cam is fast asleep. I don't know how he can drop off at a time like this. For a start, even with our arctic-grade sleeping bags it's absolutely freezing in here. But he's dead to the world.

HiM asLeep

Me
FReeZing

I wasn't supposed to be coming here until Wednesday but Mum and Dad were going to a party and Jemima was at Miriam's for a sleepover, so Mum asked Hazel if I could visit so that she and Dad could have some 'couple time'. Couple time for them probably means looking at garden shed catalogues. Anyway, it was good news for me and Cam.

We insisted on sleeping in here and not in Cam's room. Hazel thought we were mad because it's only just stopped snowing and the tree house is on a hill in the Peak District. But we figured that if we slept here, we could sneak out without being detected and go down to the village to do some investigation and that's what we've just done.

We left it until 9pm before we set off. We needed it to be dark so that we wouldn't be seen, plus Cam's mum always watches Casualty at nine and she hates being disturbed so we knew she wouldn't notice us. We crept through the garden, sliding down the grass on our coats so that our footsteps wouldn't disturb the neighbour's dog.

Once we got down to the road, we started running. Casualty is only on for an hour and Cam's mum likes us to be asleep by ten so we knew we didn't have long.

It was quiet in the village. There were cars parked outside The Crown pub and some music blaring out and there was one old couple walking dogs but otherwise no one else around. We edged along to Marsden's with our backs against the wall. The shop was shut up for the night, but when we peeped through the window we could see the door into the back room was open slightly and the light was on. Someone was definitely in there.

Cam whispered to me to follow him round the back. I don't see why I had to follow him. I'm much more like the detective in this partnership and he should be my sidekick. But, I suppose he does know the village better than me and if I'd been in charge we might have gone the wrong way and fallen into the river or something.

Plus he had the torch. So I followed him. He took us through a little housing estate and down a tiny path, then suddenly ducked down behind a wall.

US Hiding Behind the Wall ↓

I ducked down, too. There was a scraping, dragging noise down below on the other side of the wall as if something was being hauled over gravel. I must have looked as if I was going to speak because Cam shoved his hand over my mouth which was the worst thing he could do. That just made me jump and then I let out some kind of muffled scream. Then we heard a voice asking, "Is anyone there?"

Mr Marsden!!! I looked at Cam who still had his hand over my mouth. He was shaking his head. We sat as still as we possibly could, but my legs were wobbling like jelly. The cold and the fact that I was crouching down might have had something to do with it, but basically I was petrified. What was he doing? He might have a knife or even a gun...

Me with JELLY LEGS

Luckily, Mr Marsden must have thought the noise was foxes or something because then the dragging sound started again and we heard a door creak open. We peeped over the top of the wall. We could just see the old guy's back as he pulled this huge bag along the ground and over the doorstep into the back of the shop. He gave one last yank on the bag's handles and then it was inside and the door slammed shut.

We stood up then and craned our necks to try and peer through the window. We could see the back of Mr Marsden's head and shoulders. He was obviously bending down over something, but we

couldn't see the bag itself and then at one point Cam accidentally trod on a plastic bottle, which made a massive crack! Mr Marsden turned and stared out of the window. We were really worried he might come back out, but instead he just shut the blinds.

After that we couldn't get away fast enough. We've been back an hour and my heart still hasn't settled down. I can't believe Cam's managing to sleep. That's why I'm the best person to lead this investigation - I'm taking it seriously. Because things really are getting serious!

Cam and I both agree there was definitely a body in that bag. There was a bulge out to one side, which must have been an elbow or knee and it was way too heavy for him to carry. The bag was the one he had been looking at the other day in the shop. So if he has killed or kidnapped someone, it was what you call premeditated. Which means that it was planned. I definitely think we should stop calling him Mr Marsden and start calling him 'THE SUSPECT'.

So here's the evidence so far:

1. The suspect bought a bag with the intention of using it for something suspicious.
2. He's been closing up the shop and lurking in the back room.
3. He's been hanging around in graveyards.

I was going to put a fourth point about his death stare, but I think that's what they call 'inadmissable'. It didn't actually cause us to die or anything and I suppose the suspect can't help the way he looks. But even without that, it all adds up to something very dodgy.

I'm still not sure it's enough for us to call the police. Whatever he's up to, we need to catch him in the act. I've no idea how we're going to do it, but Wednesday is the day - that's if we don't freeze to death overnight.

ME as a FROZEN SNOWMAN

THURSDAY 10TH APRIL

I haven't written in here for ages, but so much has happened! On Tuesday I went to Cam's for another sleepover. Jemima is at Guide camp so it was just me and Cam. We made some notes up in the tree house in the morning. We both agree that the only way to catch Marsden in the act is to stay as close to him as possible without looking suspicious.

So, in the afternoon we pretended to be helpful and asked Cam's mum if she needed anything from the shops, then we headed down there on a recon mission. Recon stands for reconnaissance. This is what it says in my dictionary about reconnaissance...

reconnaissance *noun*
Preliminary surveying or investigation.

Military observation of a region to locate an enemy or ascertain strategic features.

Mr Marsden and his wife were both in the shop. We'd made a list of things to look out for:

1. STRANGE LOOKS BETWEEN THE SUSPECT AND THE SUSPECT'S WIFE.

2. UNUSUAL THINGS IN THE SHOP.

3. WEAPONS.

But it seemed like any normal day in a normal shop. That's often the way though. The perfectly normal façade hides all sorts of dark goings on in the background. It happens on Midsomer Murders all the time.

Anyway, we were in the shop. I swear Cameron must have turned over every apple before he chose the ones he wanted and I had read all the use-by dates on the packets of rice. Eventually Mrs Marsden came over and asked us if she could help and Cam told her we were just looking for the very best kind of rice. As if rice is that interesting. She fell for it though and said there might some basmati for curries in the back.

CAM iN the SHOP →

RICE RICE RICE

APPLES

Just as she was about to go and look in the back, Mr Marsden jumped up and said he'd go instead.

I whispered in code...

"HEGGE DEGGOSEGGN'T WEGGANT HEGGER SNEGGOOPEGGING EGGIN THEGGE BEGGACK!"

which meant...

"HE DOESN'T WANT HER SNOOPING IN THE BACK!"

We waited. After a couple of minutes Mr Marsden came back out. He didn't say much and his white face was stiff like it was made of cardboard. He'd make a good ventriloquist because his lips hardly moved when he said there was no rice in the back. I picked up a pack of the ordinary rice and wondered what else I could do to keep us in the shop.

Then Cam started talking. He looked at a box of eggs over by the counter and started asking if 'farm eggs' meant 'free range' or not. Mrs Marsden obviously thought he was being cheeky and started going on about how many years she'd been getting eggs from Snaithing Farm and how those chucks were the happiest chucks she'd ever seen.

Eventually Cam agreed to buy the eggs and Mr Marsden bagged up the food. He never smiled once. When I handed over the ten pound note that Hazel had given me, our hands touched and I swear it was like a current of electricity ran right through me! He looked me in the eye and glared at me and, for a moment, I thought he was going to grab hold of my wrist and pull me into the back room. But then he just passed me the change.

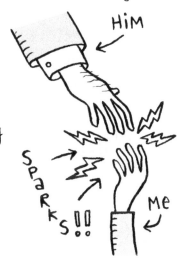

HiM

SPARKS!!

Me

We hung around the back for a bit in the afternoon, sitting on the grass behind the wall. In the daylight and with Mr Marsden out in the front, we managed to peer through the window into the back room but it was hard to see much except shelves and crates of vegetables and stuff.

At three o'clock we went back into the shop for some drinks and crisps. An hour later Mrs Marsden left and Mr Marsden shut up the shop, pulled down the blinds and went into the back room again. We made a note of the time but, as there was nothing more to see we went back home and played on Cam's computer until bedtime.

Then, yesterday... MAJOR BREAKTHROUGH!!!!!
we went back to the shop again. Mr Marsden was sitting
at the counter writing in a book and drinking a cup
of coffee. He barely even looked up when we came in.
This time we pretended we'd come for a newspaper. It
was all we could afford when we pooled the change in
our pockets. Cam went up to the counter as if he was
going to pay for the newspaper and
then he did the craziest thing. He
shoved the folded paper across the
counter, knocking the coffee all
over Mr Marsden's book.

Mr Marsden went nuts. For the first
time ever his pale face got some colour in it. Cameron
picked up the book and started flicking through the
pages and shaking it as if he was trying to get the
coffee stains off. (we tried to read it, but the pages
were full of scribbles and arrows.)

Notes, arrows, squiggles
and coffee stains

Mr Marsden leant right over the counter and snatched the book out of Cam's hands. He was screaming that it was private property and we had no business touching it. Then he literally shoved us out into the street! He's pretty strong for an old guy. I guess psycho murderers/vampires really do have super-strength.

FRIDAY 11TH APRIL

I can't believe I've been banished to my room in the holidays, all because I've been trying to save the local area from someone who could turn out to be a mass murderer! Parents suck. Now it's going to be really hard to get any further with our investigations, and who knows what might happen while I'm stuck in here? The suspect could strike again and another innocent life will be lost.

I didn't tell Mum all this because she wouldn't believe me. She'd just say I watch too much TV. I don't know why parents always side with other adults. Just because you're old, it doesn't make you right.

I'm only grounded because last night Mrs Marsden phoned up Cam's mum (who then phoned Mum) and told her we'd been upsetting Mr Marsden by hanging around the shop in a shifty way. Us, shifty! We weren't the ones with a body in a bag!

If it wasn't so unfair it would be funny.

MONDAY 14TH APRIL

It was back to school today, worse luck.
Mrs Smithers kept telling me off for staring out of the window and swinging on my chair, but it's a bit difficult to concentrate on lessons when you know there is a KILLER ON THE LOOSE. I couldn't stop thinking about how Mr Marsden had totally lost it with us over his book. Could the identity of the body in the bag lie in its pages?

When she had finished telling me off for daydreaming and politely requested that Mark Doyle stop scratching his initials onto his desk, Mrs Smithers started talking about the Family Detectives project again. We're now talking about where our families come from. Mrs Smithers reckons that if we ask our parents and grandparents we might discover that our distant relatives come from all sorts of far-off places. She's pinned a giant world map on the classroom wall. The idea is that we put ourselves on the map and then use different coloured strings to link ourselves with our relatives all over the world. I think it could end up being a right tangle, but that's just the kind of thing Mrs Smithers loves.

ALL TANGLED UP

Then this afternoon Mrs Smithers said we had to talk about how babies are made because there had been lots of giggling and shuffling about when Jemima talked about eggs and sperm the other day. She started going on about how babies grow inside the tummies of women and how they're made from the eggs from a woman and the sperm from a man. Me and Jemima have known all this stuff since infant school. You kind of need to know about eggs and sperm when you're donor conceived.

This is what it says in my 'Wonders of Science' book about how babies are made...

Reproductive System

To make a baby you need an egg or *ovum* from a woman and a sperm from a man.

Sperm are stored in a man's body.

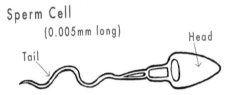

Sperm Cell
(0.005mm long)

Tail

Head

Eggs are stored in a woman's body.

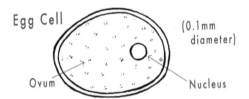

Egg Cell

(0.1mm diameter)

Ovum

Nucleus

Conception usually occurs when the sperm meets the egg inside the woman's body during sexual intercourse, but eggs can also be fertilised outside of the body and then put back in. This is called In Vitro Fertilisation or IVF.

55

When Mum and Dad talked to us about it, ages ago, they told us that usually one egg and one sperm make one baby, but sometimes you can get two eggs and two sperm coming together at the same time and that makes twins, like Jemima and me.

Sometimes you can get one egg and one sperm that split off into two and that can make twins as well. If twins come from one egg and one sperm, then they're identical twins. If there are two eggs and two sperm then they're called fraternal twins.

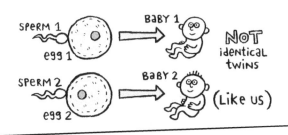

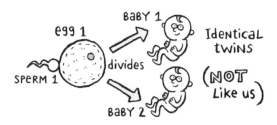

Jemima and I are fraternal twins, which doesn't make much sense because this is what it says in my dictionary...

fraternal *adjective*

Of or like a brother or brothers.

And last time I looked, Jemima was a girl, but I guess the scientific definition doesn't have anything to do with brothers.

Anyway, that's how we were made. With two eggs from an egg donor and two sperm from a sperm donor. The embryos were put inside my mum and they grew into me and Jemima and on the 11th February 2003 she gave birth to us just like any normal mum. So, even though we weren't genetically related to her, she says she felt like we were hers from way before we were born. Which is weird to think about, but kind of nice too.

The lesson seemed to shut people up anyway because no one said anything afterwards. I think they're getting bored of the whole subject. I certainly am!

z Z z Z Z Z Z

SATURDAY 19TH APRIL

We're at Jazz and Martha's today because it's Ella's eleventh birthday. She's mine and Jemima's niece but we don't get her a card which says 'Happy Birthday Niece' on it or anything, because it's pretty weird having a kid niece who's the same age as you. Michael (Jazz's brother) is here and so is Jake (Ella's genetic dad) and his partner Ben, so it's a full house.

At the moment I'm sitting on the swing in the garden writing this. I came outside because

a) I wanted a breather. I love Jazz and all that, but she's big into bear hugs and she and Martha have the loudest voices ever and sometimes coming round here is like hanging out in a hurricane.

b) I want to think about what me and Cam should do next about Mr Marsden.

c) I cannot BELIEVE what just happened! Ella just unwrapped her presents and she got an iPhone from Jake.

It's so out of order. I've been begging Mum and Dad to let me have one for ages but they say no because I already have a phone and they don't want me on the Internet. Er, no! What I actually own is a huge plastic embarrassment with numbers for 'Mum' and 'Dad' programmed in for emergencies. Also, the Internet thing is ridiculous, I mean what am I going to be looking at? I only like watching Xtreme Skateboarding Fails on YouTube! Those clips are hilarious.

Ella always gets loads of presents because she's got two mums and then her dad and his partner always buy her stuff, too. Plus, they all still have parents who are alive.

So, my dad is Ella's grandad (weird, I know) and Serene is Ella's grandma, but then she's also got four more grandmas and grandads, which is really unfair because we've only got Gramps and, no offence, but he doesn't buy the best presents. For our last birthday he gave me and Jemima matching red and white bobble hats. We looked like something out of where's wally!

Ella's dad is really cool. She doesn't call him 'Dad', she calls him 'Jake'. I asked her about that a while back and she said that her mums (she calls Jazz 'Mum' and Martha 'Mumma') are her parents - they do all the mum and dad stuff. Jake is like her uncle or something. She says he's great and she loves him, but he's different from her mums. She calls him 'Dad' to her friends though cause it's easier and means she doesn't have to answer loads of silly questions. I totally get that!

Jake lives in Manchester and Ella gets to go there sometimes on weekends. We went over to visit once. He has this amazing apartment near a river. It's all glass and steel like something from a movie. I'm not sure what Jake does, but he always dresses really cool, in jeans and leather jackets, not like my dad, who today is wearing an old pair of jogging bottoms. When we got here, Jazz raised her eyebrows at him, but he just winked at her and said "It's all about comfort sweetheart - got to have room for all this delicious food."

MY dad   ELLa's dad

Dad's got a point about the food. It's the best thing about parties at Ella's house. Jazz makes the most amazing spicy jerk chicken. I asked her how come it's so yummy and no one else can make it like her even though Mum and Dad do give it a go. She said it's an

Jamaica

old Jamaican recipe that has been passed down through generations. I guess Jazz or Serene would be good to interview for the family detectives thing and then I could put a pin in Jamaica.

During lunch everyone started talking about our family and where we come from and how different we all look. Serene explained how people including her parents came over from the Caribbean in the fifties to find work. Mum said how we're all immigrants really and although our donors might have been English, people with blonde hair and blue eyes were probably originally from Scandinavia so our genes might be Norwegian or Swedish and we could be descended from Vikings!

Ella wanted to know who is responsible for her looks. She has light brown skin, but red curly hair. Jake told her that the red curls came from his granny in Ireland. Then he made Ella cringe by singing some soppy Irish song. All of the grown-ups joined in. They were off on one and there was nothing to do, but get stuck in to the jerk chicken.

It's one in the morning and I'm now on the airbed in Jazz and Martha's living room. It got so late in the end that Mum and Dad said Jemima and me could stay over. Jemima is sleeping in Ella's room. It's a bit spooky down here on my own. I just can't stop thinking about Mr Marsden and his weird, piercing eyes and the body in the bag. What if there are more bodies? What if, while everyone is sleeping, he is out prowling for his next victim?

I'm really worried. We've really got the suspect rattled now. He knows the net is closing in. What if he goes after Cam? If only I had that iPhone - I could just send him a message.

I'm home now. Can't wait to spend tonight back in my own bed. Ella's cat jumped on my airbed in the night and it went completely flat overnight, which is probably why I woke up so early. Jazz and Martha were in the kitchen so I asked them if I could make a phone call. I really wanted to check Cam hadn't been murdered by Mr Marsden. I didn't realise it was only seven in the morning.

Hazel wasn't best pleased when I called. She said Cam was still in bed and no, she wasn't going to wake him up and yes, she was sure he was there. She did go and check though, and he was fine. I felt a bit silly then, so I just said I'd phone later and hung up.

Before Dad arrived to collect us, I had time to interview Jazz for the Family Detectives project. Jemima didn't get up until nine, so she missed out. She was really annoyed when she clocked me with the voice recorder. This is the interview transcript:

Interview commenced: 08:00
Sunday 20th April

"So, Jazz. How are we related?"

"Hmm, that's a tough one to start with. If you weren't donor conceived, we'd be half brother and sister, but I don't like all that half stuff, so I guess you're mine and Michael's little brother and Jemima is our little sister."

"Yeah, it's like with Ryan. I don't call him my half brother."

"He's just your big teenage pain-in-the-butt brother, right?"

"So, what did you think when my mum and dad told you that they were going to use donor conception to have me and Jemima. Did they tell you straight away?"

"Now that is a funny story because they didn't say anything at first. I knew they'd thought about having kids and that they weren't quick in coming along but it's not really the kind of thing you talk to your dad about a lot. Which is where it gets crazy because, while they were going to the clinic to conceive you guys, Martha and I were hatching plans with our friend Jake. And we didn't mention it either. So, by the time your mum told me she was pregnant, I was pregnant too, with Ella. We should all have just come out with it much sooner."

"Wasn't it a bit weird having a child at the same time as your dad?"

"It was a bit strange but, you know what? I love my dad and he loves your mum and I just wanted him to be happy. And, do you know what else? That's all your dad wanted for me and it's all he wants for you, too. Probably he didn't expect me to fall in love with Martha and didn't expect us to have Ella using our friend Jake as a sperm donor, but life doesn't always turn out the way you expect. And if it did, we wouldn't get all the lovely surprises that come along."

"Like me and Jemima?"

"Of course. Your mum and dad were over the moon when they had you. I've never seen two people happier. They thought they were the luckiest people alive. And so they were, my love, so they were. You're a gem. Both of you are."

"And Ella's not bad either."

"Ella-Bella is the love of my life, believe me. There's no greater joy than being a parent, doesn't matter how the child is conceived."

"Thanks Jazz."

"Is that the end of the interview?"

"I think I've got what I...."

Interview terminated at 08:17 due to bear hug.

TUESDAY 22ND APRIL

Sometimes me and Hamid take our skateboards and go in the park after school. We only have to cross one road to get there so Mum and Dad don't mind us going off on our own so long as we're home for tea. You're not really supposed to skate in the park but no one takes any notice. There's a neat little bridge where you can do tricks and we're trying to practice skating up and down the steps on this old monument to Queen Victoria.

Today we skated to the new parkour area. Mostly it's just little kids hanging off the railings but today there were a few big lads from the local comp doing proper free-running tricks. They looked pretty cool bouncing off the walls and swinging around.

A big guy wearing a bandana on his head swung from one bar to another and, for a moment, I could just imagine he was a gorilla swinging on the branches of a tree. All he needed was a banana in one hand and the picture would have been perfect. I told Ham and he said that made sense because, technically we are all descended from apes.

It's funny when you think about it. This whole 'where do we come from?' thing that Mrs Smithers goes on about. Forget Jamaica or Scandinavia or whatever. We all come from the jungle! Kind of makes the whole donor business seem a bit insignificant. It made me wonder how many generations you have to go back before you find an ape in the family. Then I thought of Gramps. I told Hamid and he laughed and started jumping around making "ooh, ooh" ape noises and banging his fists on his chest.

"My name's Gramps Nolan and I'm a Neanderthal," he said.

The big guy with the bandana swung off the bar and landed on the ground in front of us.

"Oi, squid," he said. "Who are you calling a Neanderthal?"

I was a bit nervous then, especially when bandana man's mates skated up to see what was going on, but Hamid is surprisingly cool in these kinds of situations.

He just changed the subject and started asking the guys how they did their moves. Bandana man looked at him like he wasn't sure whether Hamid was laughing at him or was genuinely impressed. Then he said, "watch and learn, kid."

We both nodded seriously and stood and watched for a while, trying not to laugh. They were just a load of monkeys showing off. Gotta admit they did look kind of cool though.

WEDNESDAY 23RD APRIL

Today in Family Detectives we were discussing what makes a

We tried lots of different definitions. If we had an idea we had to come up and write it on the whiteboard, then the rest of the class had to decide if the idea made sense.

Hamid said that a family is, "a group of people who live together in one house." But Helena Pilkington said that her older brother is at university and he lives with a house of friends, so that was no good.

She said that maybe a family is a group of people that contains a mum and a dad and some children. But then Miriam said no because it's just her and her mum slash auntie at home, but that they're still a family.

Miriam said it might be a group of people who are related who live together in a house, but then Callum Reese said that couldn't be right because his mum lives with his stepdad in one house and his dad and his stepmum live in another house and he and his brother live in both houses at different times.

So, then Callum said that a family must be a group of genetically related people and that whether or not they lived in the same house doesn't matter.

I was surprised by how angry that made me feel. I don't normally put my hand up for anything, but this time I even beat Jemima to it. I told Mrs Smithers that that couldn't be right because by that logic, adopted children wouldn't be family and Jemima and I would be part of a family that we've never met and are never going to meet. And that wouldn't even be a family because the donors don't even know each other. My family is me and

Jemima and Mum and Dad and Ryan and Jazz and Martha and Ella and Michael and Gramps. Definitely.

Mrs Smithers asked me what my definition would be and in the end I came up with this: Family are the people who love you and care about you and who you can rely on. Some of the class made silly 'ah' noises when I said it, but Mrs. Smithers liked it.

Then Abusammed put his hand up. He doesn't talk a lot in class, I think cause he's worried he might say the wrong words, although his English is getting really good now.

ABUSAMMED

He said "No!" Just like that, and shook his head. Everyone stared. Mrs Smithers asked him what he meant and he said, "My father dead. Still family."

It was a really good point. You could tell Mrs Smithers loved it because she was nodding so hard her dangly earrings were rattling.

"Family carries on being family even when people die," she said. "I wonder if we could change your definition

Archie, to take account of that?"

So I tried again. I said, "Family are the people who love you and care about you and who you feel connected to."

Mrs Smithers turned around to write it on the board, but then Jemima asked whether parents who don't look after their children properly are still family.

"I don't think so," I said. "Not according to our definition. By law they might be called family, but I think you should only be able to call yourself family if you're loving and caring. You can be genetically-related or you can live together, but family should be about connection and love and care - even if you don't get it right all the time."

And so that was our class definition.

I THINK IT'S A GOOD ONE

THURSDAY 24TH APRIL

Ha! In your face Jemima swotty Nolan, with your hundred interviews including your sneaky one with Cam who FYI is _my_ best friend. Wait till you hear about the bonus interview I've just done with another DC girl - someone you haven't even met!

Mum's still plotting about going to this DC conference and while she's been looking into it, she's come across another DC family in Sheffield called the Braithwaites. There's a mum and a dad, (can't remember their names) and they've got one daughter Poppy, who was conceived by egg donation.

They all came round for a cup of tea after school tonight. Jemima had choir practice so I had to hang out with Poppy and BOY can that girl talk! So I decided to interview her. This is what I got...

POPPY

Interview commenced: 16:30
Thursday 24th April

"Thanks for letting me interview you about your family, Poppy."

"That's fine, Archie. I like talking about my family. Mum calls me 'Little Miss Chatterbox', she says I said my first word at six months old. Apparently the teachers at my nursery taught me to say, "Poppy is a genius" when I was just one! I can speak three languages. Not fluently, but I'm pretty good. Maybe I take after my dad a bit because he's a linguistics professor at the university."

"So, you're genetically-related to your dad, but not to your mum? Do you think that changes your relationship with her?"

"Not really. If anything I get on better with my mum. And Mum says that because she carried me and gave birth to me, she'd already bonded with me way before I was born. She says before she had me, she was really worried that she wouldn't like me or that she'd want to send me back when I was naughty, but she says she took one look at me and knew she'd love me forever."

"I wonder how your dad felt about it?"

"Well, that's funny, because Mum says that it took her ages to persuade Dad to use an egg donor. She says that he really wanted to have her child and thought it might be weird to have a child that wasn't my mum's. But then, when they had me, it wasn't like he was having another woman's child because my mum was the one who was pregnant and she was the one looking after me."

"So, you're only nine and you were conceived after 2005 which means you'll have an identifiable donor. Do you think you'll want to meet them when you're eighteen?"

"I think I might. It's not like I'd want another mum because one mum is more than enough and my mum's great. I suppose I'm just the kind of person that likes to know everything so I'd like to see where I came from. It would be useful when I'm older, just to know about any health risks and stuff like that."

"Do you think your mum would mind?"

"That's the tricky bit because I think she would. She says that whatever I decide is OK with her, but I can tell it makes her feel funny. I suppose she thinks I might meet my donor and get on really well and then decide that I want spend all my time with her or something. But I might only want to meet them once. My mum is my real mum. It's hard though to get grown-ups to see things sometimes, isn't it?"

"Yep. Thanks Poppy,"

"You're welcome. Is that it? Because I've got some more to say about..."

Interview terminated at 16.45 due to tape running out.

FRIDAY 25TH APRIL

 hoops, doughnut stains! I'll have to write around them.

I've just been eating the last of the doughnuts Mum bought for tea last night. She got loads of them, but there was only one left over after Poppy had finished stuffing her face. I swear she ate four doughnuts in five minutes. Anyway, now I'm thinking about dozy Danny Saunders mixing up doughnuts and donors again. It was pretty funny and I suppose there are some similarities. Doughnuts come in lots of varieties and so do donors.

These are some of the types of doughnuts you can have:

1) Sugar and jam - like the one I've just stuffed down.
2) Iced with sprinkles - a bit girly really, but still very edible.
3) Chocolate - also tasty.
4) Custard - King of Doughnuts and my personal fave.

These are some of the types of donations donors can make:

SPERM DONATION - where a family uses a donor's sperm to fertilise the mother's egg.

EGG DONATION - where a family uses the donor's eggs but they are fertilised by the father's sperm.

DOUBLE DONATION - that's me. Egg and sperm are used from a male and a female donor who are unconnected.

EMBRYO DONATION - when an egg has already been fertilised by sperm it is called an embryo. Often embryos are left over from IVF treatment. The ones that weren't used are sometimes donated to another family.

Lots of families get eggs, sperm or embryos at clinics close to home. This is what my parents did, but you can visit other countries, or import them, like Cam's mum did. Some people go to Europe, some to the US or other countries. In the US, all clinics give lots of information about donors, although most donors are anonymous.

Some families think that by going abroad where they have lots more information available, they'll be able to choose what kind of kid they'll get. In my opinion, that's not necessarily going to work because even if you inherit someone's genes you're not going to be exactly like them - look at Jacob Taylor and his footballer Grandad. Still, I guess if my parents had done that they might have been able to choose donors who weren't shortsighted and I wouldn't be a speccy science nerd - I'd just be a science nerd instead.

And donors can also be:
⭐ Known (like Jazz and Martha's friend, Jake).
⭐ Unknown and identifiable (like Poppy's egg donor).
⭐ Unknown and anonymous (like mine and Jemima's donors

A known donor is when the donor is actually known to the family. This can work really well (like with Jazz and Martha and Jake), but it can also be a bit complicated because there's no law about how much involvement the known donor can have with the child.

Cameron's mum Hazel told him that before she decided to import sperm from the States to make Cameron, a friend of hers said that he would help her to have a child. But then she wasn't sure that she wanted this guy to be hanging around all the time and in the end she decided that she'd rather just bring Cam up on her own. But some single mothers and lesbian families like having a father figure around for their children. And sometimes, the known donor doesn't actually end up having any more to do with the children than an unknown donor.

Unknown donors are what mum and dad used to make me and Jemima. You get the sperm or eggs from a clinic and you don't know who the actual donors are. Unknown donors can vary too because they can be either 'identifiable' or 'anonymous', and this can depend on when the donation was made and in which country. Identifiable donors are ones that can be tracked down, like when detectives identify the murderer in a story.

Anonymous donors are the ones that we can't find, like when someone sends a letter without signing it. In the UK, the law changed in 2005. So donors who donated before 2005 are anonymous and after 2005 they are identifiable. Since 2005, all donors sign papers to say that they agree to any children that they're genetically related to being able to find them once they're eighteen. So, Poppy Braithwaite will be able to trace her identifiable donor, but Jemima and I won't. I don't know how I feel about that really. I mean, I'm not that bothered at the moment cause I've got a mum and dad. I guess I might be more curious in the future. I don't know.

I started thinking about all the different combinations of donors and families you could have and it went on and on.

Hamid spent ages working it out and he reckons there are probably about 128 different combinations, which, when you think about it, probably makes donor conceived children even more varied than doughnuts.

donor conceived kids

doughnuts

Although, when I Googled it, I came up with this site for Dunkin' Donuts in the States and they apparently have 69 different types of doughnuts in their shop. Which makes me think I need to persuade Mum and Dad that we need a holiday in Florida ASAP!

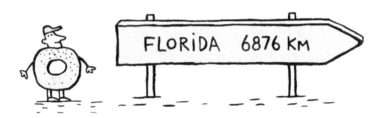

FLORIDA 6876 KM

SATURDAY 26TH APRIL

Mum and Dad brought up the conference again this morning. They are trying to trick me into going by telling me that Cam will be there. I don't think so! He's about as interested in sitting around discussing donor conception as I am!

Dad did say me and Cam might be able to share a hotel room though. I didn't realise the conference is in London, or that we would be staying overnight - which I have to admit would be quite cool. Mum even said we might be able to go to the Science Museum on the Sunday. Although I don't see why she and dad can't just take me straight there instead of to the stupid conference.

Jemima started jumping around at the idea of being able to do even more interviews with other donor conceived children. When mum said that the main session in the morning was a panel discussion with donor conceived teenagers and she might be able to record it, she practically passed out.

Jemima just kept going on about how it would be amazing for the Family Detectives Project. I wiped the smile of her face by telling her we will have finished the project by then and guess what she said? That Mrs Smithers thinks the project has been so interesting that we may even carry it on after half term.

nooooooooooooo !

IIF THERE IS NO MORE WRITING IN THIS BOOK IT'S BECAUSE I'VE JUMPED OFF A CLIFF!

TELL ME about YOUR family, ARCHIE.

MRS SMITHERS   ME →

Me again! I'm not off a cliff, I'm at Cam's but I'm writing in my diary because Cam is being really boring and is on his computer looking up stuff about climbing sites in California.

I thought we were going to be investigating Mr Marsden. Mum and Hazel and Jemima have gone out for a walk and afternoon tea, so this is the ideal opportunity, but instead the curse of the Family Detectives Project has struck again and now Cam's been sucked in. He says our school project has got him thinking about his donor, who came from California.

Cam's donor was anonymous too - his sperm was sent from America over to the UK clinic Cam's mum used. Cam won't be able to trace his donor, but his mum's told him she has a special donor number and that whenever Cam's ready, they might be able to trace any half-siblings through the Donor Sibling Registry in the US.

So now Cam's all excited about a possible future trip to California. Cam's mum has told him that besides being 'clever' his donor is 'tall' and 'of athletic build', so Cam reckons his donor could be a climber and that's why Cam is good at climbing. He thinks his half-siblings might be into climbing, too.

If you ask me, he's getting a bit ahead of himself thinking that because he knows his donor is 'tall' and 'athletic' that he and all his offspring must be climbers. I didn't say anything though.

I just hope Cam hurries up so we can go out and carry on our detective work. My hands keep sweating when I think about Mr Marsden and the body in the bag. I've been watching the news a lot to see if anyone's been reported missing, but nothing so far. Maybe the victim didn't have anyone to report them missing. What if it's an old person - or a tramp or something?

The evidence is really stacking up and I think we're not far from solving this mystery. After all, detectives on TV are always saying stuff like, 'You can't solve a murder without a body!' Well that's the one thing we do have - a body! We know exactly where it's being kept and who has hidden it. We just don't know whose body it is!

SUNDAY 27TH APRIL

I'm back home with Jemima and Mum, but I literally do not know what to do with myself. I haven't been able to sleep and when I do, I just dream of being chased by Mr Marsden. He's still on the loose and after yesterday we're 100% absolutely, totally, no doubt whatsoever, certain that he is a KILLER. The trouble is we can't even report it to the police.

When Cam eventually switched off the computer yesterday afternoon, we went off to the village to check on the suspect.

This time we went straight to the back of the shop. After the phone call from Mrs Marsden we were under strict instructions to stay away, but we could hardly just give up on the whole investigation, not when we were so close.

The blind on the window was down and we couldn't see what was going on inside, so we sat down behind the wall opposite the shop's back door to wait and see if anyone would come in or out. We opened a pack of Fruit Pastilles and occupied ourselves by coming up with ways to get out of the conference.

REASONS CAMERON AND ARCHIE CAN SADLY NOT ATTEND THE CONFERENCE:

1. They are trapped under some heavy furniture in Ryan's room.

2. They are attending a climbing masterclass in California.

3. They are allergic to group discussions.

4. It is against their religion to travel south of Birmingham.

5. They have been hacked to death by a murdering grocer.

I was just telling Cameron about Poppy Braithwaite when we heard the back door opening and then the sound of footsteps on the gravel.

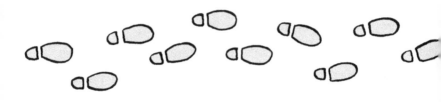

The footsteps stopped and then there was a squeak, followed by the sound of running water. We needed to see what was going on so we knelt up to peep over the wall.

It was the suspect! He had his back to us and was leaning down towards an outdoor tap, scrubbing and scrubbing at his hands. A river of red water was flowing onto the ground and towards the drain. Blood. Mr Marsden was washing blood off his hands!

After that we just bolted. We didn't want to hang around in case he saw us. I'm going to stop calling him the suspect now because we no longer suspect he's a psycho-killer. We KNOW he's a psycho-killer.

We sat in the playground trying to work out what to do next. We thought about telling our mums but, as Cam pointed out, you don't see Sherlock Holmes and watson running off to their parents. And anyway, we knew they'd be mad at us for stalking a harmless old man again even though we've seen proper evidence, with the body bag and the blood and everything.

In the end we went straight to the police. The police station in Cam's village is nothing like the big glass ones you see on TV, with the rows of cop cars outside. It's just a brown stone house, like all the other brown stone houses. You can only tell it's a police station by the small blue sign outside.

THE POLICE Station

POLICE SIGN

Anyway, Cam had just pushed the door to go in when I spotted Mr Marsden through the glass, standing there in his long black coat, no handcuffs or anything, chatting to the police sergeant like he had nothing to hide. In fact, they looked like they were the best of friends.

Because the door was ajar we could hear every word. "Never seen or heard of again," Mr Marsden was saying in his raspy voice. And then the officer tapped his finger against his nose and said, "Leave it with me, George. I can help."

And so we legged it, before they saw us. There was nothing else to be done because obviously

THE POLICE ARE IN ON IT TOO!!!!

We found Hazel and Mum and Jemima in Jinty's Café having tea with Hazel's friend, Sarah. We must have looked really odd though, because straight away Hazel and Mum started asking us what was wrong and what we'd been doing. When we said nothing, Hazel said we both looked very pale and kept feeling Cam's head for a temperature. In the end the only way I could distract them was to ask Hazel and Sarah for an interview. I let Jemima do all the talking.

THE MUMS FUSSING OVER CAM

MONDAY 28TH APRIL

Here's yesterday's interview. I've only just finished typing it up. Normally on a Monday night I'd be watching a re-run of Quincy, but the last thing I wanted to think about was crime. I needed something to take my mind off what we saw yesterday.

Interview commenced at 15:42, Sunday 27th April in Jinty's Café, Hathersage.

Jemima: So, Sarah, you're Hazel's best friend, aren't you? How long have you known each other?

Sarah: I've known Hazel since I was eleven. We were at school together.

Jemima: What was she like?

Sarah: She was one of those really annoying people who was good at everything and didn't have to try. She used to copy my homework and somehow get better marks!

Hazel: I did not.

Sarah: You so did. You used to copy my French homework every morning and then you got an A in your exam and I got a C.

Hazel: Sorry.

Jemima: Do you remember when Hazel decided to have Cameron, Sarah?

Sarah: I do. She'd just broken up with this guy, Chris. He wasn't right for her and he had never been clear about whether he wanted children or not. By then she was in her late thirties and the rest of us already had kids. I remember her being really sad around that time.

Hazel: Yeah. I was trying to make it work with Chris because of the children thing, but I just couldn't do it in the end, because he wouldn't decide one way or the other and I wanted to get on with starting a family. I thought I'd missed my chance when I left him. It was heartbreaking for me.

Jemima: What made you decide to use a donor?

Hazel: It was a big decision. I just realised that I wasn't going to be happy if I didn't have a child.

Sarah: She's one of those people who will go after what she wants. It was tricky for her though. We all thought she was mad.

Jemima: Why?

Sarah: Well, it's hard raising a child on your own. It's not for everyone. And in our circle of friends it was unusual.

Hazel: It was hard. I guess it still is. In some ways the hardest part was when Cam was about five and he started to say he wanted a dad. Partly because his friends had dads and he felt different. But maybe he also wanted a man in his life, or wanted me to have a husband. I don't know. We talked about it and I never told him he was wrong to feel like that. He'd say it sometimes when the kids at school had asked him stupid questions and he couldn't make them understand. Whenever that happened we'd cheer each other up with a good movie and talk about all the things we could be happy about. My dad was really helpful and spends lots of time with Cam. He's much closer to Cam than he would have been if I'd had a partner, I think. Recently Cam's been saying that he's so glad to have me and his grandad that he doesn't really think about not having a dad.

Jemima: When you hear that, Sarah, do you still think Hazel did the right thing?

Sarah: Oh, definitely! As soon as she was pregnant I knew it was the right thing for her. She was so happy. And, of course, once we saw Cameron... well, who couldn't love that boy? And she's been a great mum to him.

Hazel: Aw. Thank you. That means a lot.

Sarah: Well, it's true. He's fabulous.

Jemima: Are you still glad you did it, Hazel?

Hazel: Absolutely! Having Cameron is the best thing I ever did. Although, when I won Businesswoman of the Year, that was a good moment, too! And that holiday in the Caribbean was nice...

Sarah: Listen to her. Still showing off, even now!

Hazel: You love me, really.

Sarah: Whatever.

Interview terminated at 16:03 due to grown-up women hugging and kissing each other.

TUESDAY 29TH APRIL

Until today the whole Marsden business has been just between me and Cam, but it feels like the situation is spiralling a bit out of control and I really needed someone to talk to about it. So after school I swore Ham to secrecy. He is really good at thinking stuff through and he said, "Flippin' 'eck, Arch!" Then he got a piece of paper and divided everything we've discovered into two columns, like this...

A BIT DODGY	VERY DODGY
Mr Marsden looks like a vampire.	He hangs around in graveyards.
He gives death-stares.	He has a body in a bag.
His touch is ice cold.	He has blood-covered hands.
He writes in a book he doesn't want to share.	He's in cahoots with the police.
He puts the CLOSED sign up when his wife is not there.	

As Ham helpfully pointed out, it's not enough for a conviction. We need more solid evidence. And the only way we're going to get more evidence is to get into the back of the shop and take pictures of the body and whatever else is in there.

I suggested Ham should come with us to distract
Mr Marsden in the front of the shop while Cameron
and I got into the back. Hamid would be perfect.
He's great at talking to people
and no one would ever suspect him
of being up to anything because
he just looks so polite and good.
But then he pointed out that even
though he would love to
be involved, there was no way his
mum would let him come all the
way on the train.

angelic Ham

Just as we were wondering what to do, Jemima appeared
on the path in front of us. Sometimes it's like Hamid
has some kind of magic power because I swear he just
conjured her out of thin air in order to tell me that
Jemima was the answer to the problem. I wasn't sure
about letting her in on the secret, but then Ham said,
"Come on. Who can you trust if not your own sister?"

He had a point. Jemima can be annoying, but she's
never actually told on me or anything like that. She
can keep a secret. So I told her. I told her everything.
And I'm glad I did because now we have a plan. Just
six days to go and then it will all be exposed.
And Cameron and I will be heroes!

SATURDAY 3RD MAY

IF YOU ARE READING THIS DIARY THEN YOU ARE PROBABLY HOLDING THE PROPERTY OF A DEAD PERSON. I'M WRITING THIS IN THE BACK ROOM OF MARSDEN'S GROCERY STORE IN HATHERSAGE. I'M WITH MY FRIEND CAMERON AND WE ARE HIDING IN FEAR OF OUR LIVES! IF YOU START AT THE BEGINNING OF THIS DIARY (SKIP THROUGH THE STUFF ABOUT MY SCHOOL PROJECT) YOU WILL SEE WHAT HAS BEEN GOING ON BUT IN A NUTSHELL WE HAVE DISCOVERED A MURDER AND WE HAVE COME TO TRY AND EXPOSE THE TRUTH ABOUT THE KILLER - MR MARSDEN. BUT NOW WE ARE STUCK IN HERE AND AAAARGH CAM JUST TRIPPED OVER THE BODY IN THE BAG AND WE CAN HEAR FOOTSTEPS...

SUNDAY 4TH MAY

It's eleven pm. This is going to be a long one and I'm tired cause we only just got home, but I'll see how far I can get.

Yesterday Mum and Dad let me and Jemima catch the train out to Hathersage to see Cameron. They were off to browse yet another garden centre (YAWN), so they didn't mind us not being with them and Dad said it would 'stop the whole trip becoming a WHINGE-A-THON'.

Cameron met us at the station and we walked into the village and round to the back of Marsden's. We went the long way round, like we've done before, so as not to be too visible. But instead of stopping at the back wall, where we usually hide, which has a long drop down to the yard on the other side, we headed round to a bit where there was a hole in the fence, which looked easier to climb through.

Jemima was still wittering about whether we were being stupid and that she didn't want to get caught, but Cam calmed her down and told her all she had to do was go into the shop and keep Mr Marsden talking. This, as I pointed out, is Jemima's best talent. She wasn't happy, but she went in.

we counted to thirty so Jemima would have enough time to get round to the shop entrance and then we went through the fence into the back yard. It was empty and everything was quiet except for the odd drip from the tap where Marsden had washed away the blood. we had reached the door and were just wondering whether we could fit through the window, which was ajar, when we heard...

"Just a tick love, I'm out back."

STINKY

It was Mrs Marsden. We quickly ran behind the big wheelie bins and held our breath as the back door opened. Mrs Marsden came out and dumped a couple of plastic crates outside. Then she went back in.

We stood up carefully and couldn't believe it. She'd left the back door open, just a crack. That solved the issue of how to get inside.

So we came out from behind the bins - which was a massive relief, because it really stank of mouldy cabbage and rotten eggs - and edged our way along the wall and into the back room of the shop on tiptoe. The room was dark and musty, piled high with tins and crates and cardboard boxes. I knocked a pile of boxes with my foot and held my breath, hoping that nothing would fall.

I could hear Jemima talking to Mrs Marsden about the price of vegetables and how supermarkets are destroying village shops. That's another thing my sister is good at - chatting to people about all sorts of nonsense. Then we heard Mrs Marsden asking Jemima to tell her parents to come in and sign the petition against the new megastore that was opening nearby.

This gave Cameron and me the chance to look around and it was then that we saw it - a giant whiteboard with scribbled notes in red pen and photos and post-it notes and newspaper cuttings stuck all over it. There were bits of coloured string connecting up the photos and dates and names scrawled across the whiteboard.

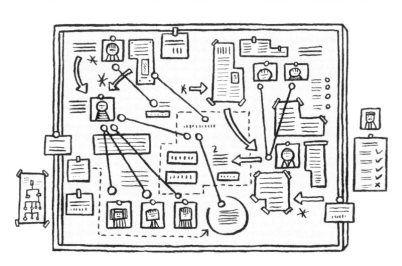

This was it! The evidence we needed. The killer's shrine to his victims with all the information recorded on one wall! Cam was obviously thinking exactly the same thing, because he took out his mobile and started taking shots of the board straight away.

We'd been there about five minutes when we heard Jemima say, "I seem to have forgotten my purse", in a very loud voice, which was the agreed signal to warn us to get out. That was when things started to go wrong. Cam decided to take one more picture and text it to Ham to show him what we'd found.

While texting he stumbled backwards right over the holdall then landed right on top of it. He was sitting right on top of the dead body! I pictured muscles squelching and blood oozing. His face looked petrified when he realised.

I held out my hand to help him up, but before we could do anything we heard Mrs Marsden say, "George, can you take over for a while? I'm just popping over to Barbara's." And then there was the sound of the shop door being locked. We were alone. With Mr Marsden, aka. the Killer.

We scrambled behind a load of boxes, but then realized we'd put ourselves even further from the back door. We started to panic then. I wrote yesterday's message thinking it would be my last ever diary entry. Cam just

sat there biting his nails. Then
another terrible thing happened.
Hamid replied to Cam's text!
Cam's phone wasn't on silent.
And his phone plays the
'Doctor who' theme tune even for
a text message. And then Mr Marsden
was standing at the door with
a knife in his hand.

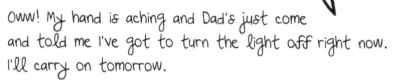

Oww! My hand is aching and Dad's just come
and told me I've got to turn the light off right now.
I'll carry on tomorrow.

TUESDAY 6TH MAY

I haven't had time to write since Sunday night
because Mum's been keeping me busy round the house.
I think I might be grounded for the rest of my life.

So, I don't know if I'm relieved or happy or disappointed.
Maybe a bit of all three. But it turns out Mr Marsden
isn't a murderer (or even a vampire) after all.

When I saw him in the shop doorway with that knife
I've never been so scared in my whole life. I was
convinced he was going to chop us into pieces and put

us in matching holdalls. Cam was terrified, too. He won't admit it, but he screamed. Proper loud and high, like Jemima when there's a spider in the bath. He said that it was me screaming, but it DEFINITELY was NOT.

SCRRREEEEEaM

Mr Marsden leapt past me and Cam and bolted the back door. He put the knife down on a shelf and lumbered towards us with his arms outstretched. Me and Cam were scrabbling around in a mad panic. Loads of tins were falling off the shelves on top of us and Mr Marsden yelled 'I'm going to kill you two...'

We started pleading with him then and Cam was crying. I just had some storeroom dust in my eyes, which is why they were watering so much.

Mr Marsden looked furious, but also a bit confused and he lunged towards us and grabbed us by the ears, which took us by surprise. It was a bit weird and very painful. Then suddenly his wife was there - with Jemima, who'd run off to fetch her.

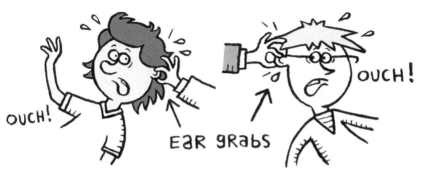

OUCH!

OUCH!

EaR gRabs

It took a while for everything to calm down and for Mr Marsden to understand that we weren't trying to rob his shop and for us to realise that he wasn't actually going to kill us. He said it was a figure of speech because he was sick of us causing chaos.

I said, "Oh yeah, then why did you come at us with a massive knife?" And do you know what he said?

"I've been on the cheese counter, cutting up a stilton, you daft lad!"

Stilton cheese →

I could have killed Jemima then. She started laughing and going on about how we were 'just two silly little boys playing detective'.

At that point, PC Davis arrived - he'd been alerted to what he described as 'a disturbance' in the grocer's. He wanted to know exactly what we'd been detecting, so we told him about the body in the bag and showed him where it was lying.

He asked if he could take a look and Mr Marsden said, "Be my guest, Jim." PC Davis hesitated a second and then leant down to inspect the massive, bulging holdall.

"I suppose you could call it a body," Mr Marsden said as the policeman slowly unzipped the bag. "A body of work, that is."

We stared in horror at the contents of the bag. There was no rotting corpse in sight, just piles and piles of folders and files and books. No wonder it was so heavy! Then Mr Marsden explained how he'd been working for months trying to trace his family tree.

"Rosalind got sick of all the clutter at home, didn't you, dear?" he said, turning to Mrs Marsden, who nodded. "So I brought all my research here." I have to sneak off into the storeroom to do some more work on it whenever Ros is out of the shop."

Mrs Marsden looked a bit annoyed at hearing that, but I was so embarrassed I couldn't speak. Cam still wasn't giving up though. I think he was just trying to make us look less like total idiots. "But what about the hanging about in graveyards," he said, "<u>and</u> we caught you washing blood off your hands. Are you going to deny that?"

For a second Mr Marsden looked totally flawed and then he reached over to the ledge at the bottom of the whiteboard. That's when we saw that we'd really got the wrong end of the stick! The red stuff wasn't blood. It was ink - from the leaky red marker pen he'd been using on his board... which wasn't full of information about victims at all, but about family members Mr Marsden was trying to trace. That's why he'd been in the graveyard too. He'd been looking for his relatives' tombstones.

As we stood there turning redder and redder, something happened to Mr Marsden's face. It cracked into something that resembled a smile. Well a sort of a sneery-smile (he still looked really annoyed) and then PC Davis burst out laughing. Mr Marsden had been asking if any of the officers who'd lived and worked in the area for years remembered anything useful about his family and the

Sergeant had promised to help by asking around the station. No wonder PC Davis found it all so funny - he knew all about Mr Marsden's genealogical research!

So there we are. Mystery solved. Thankfully Mr Marsden didn't want to press charges, although he did phone Mum tonight. I don't know exactly what was said, but they were on the phone for ages and afterwards she came up to my room and said we needed to pay him back for all the stress that we'd caused. Judging by the look on Mum's face, we might be helping Mr Marsden out for a VERY long time..

ONE FURIOUS MUM

THURSDAY 8TH MAY

In class today we tied ourselves in knots with the bits of string, looking at where everyone comes from. Going back a few generations, Mrs Smithers was right about there being connections all over the world. We didn't bother with the donor stuff for the map but even without that we could put a string across to Jamaica and one to the States because that's where

Hippy John is from. And one of Dad's grandparents came from Scotland, too.

Then Mrs Smithers told us about the 'six degrees of separation' theory. Apparently, some guy called Frigyes Karinthy (great name!) came up with this idea that everyone is only six steps away from knowing everyone in the world. So, let's say there was a kid called Archie living in San Francisco, I would know somebody who would know somebody else who would know somebody else who would know somebody else who would know somebody else who would know the American Archie!

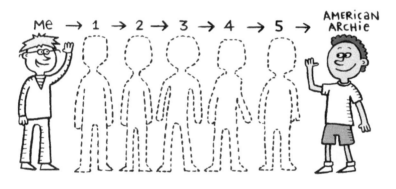

Mrs Smithers reckons that we're all connected and all part of one big world family. Which is all very well as a theory, but in real life it doesn't always feel that way. I might only have six degrees of separation from all the random human beings on the planet, but I feel a million miles away from the people who donated the eggs and sperm to make me.

I've never really minded being donor conceived before, but then I've never spent that much time thinking about it until now. And lately I've started wondering what my donors are like.

Maybe they were some really cool, glamorous people and they're still out there living cool, glamorous lives with their own children. I saw this Olympic yachtsman on telly and for some reason I started thinking that maybe he was my sperm donor. He was tall and blonde and tanned and he'd sailed round the world on a yacht.
And then I looked at Dad and he seemed a bit old and ordinary.

OLYMPIC dad

MY dad

And my egg donor might be a film star or something. Maybe she lives in a mansion with servants. I mean, Mum's great and all that, but when she was nagging at me to tidy my room yesterday I found myself thinking that my egg donor would probably have a cleaner to tidy up for me and that she would definitely buy me an iPhone.

STRICT NAGGING MUM

FOR ARCHIE

HOLLYWOOD MUM

But then, yesterday I heard Ryan shouting, "I wish you weren't my mother!" at Mum - who must have been having a go at him about his room, as usual. It made me feel a bit sad because I do kind of wish that Mum and Dad had just been like everyone else and that they were my genetic parents. I know I'm not making sense. One minute I wish I had glamorous parents and the next I wish my boring mum and dad were my genetic ones. It's just all a bit confusing right now.

Anyway, I suppose I shouldn't hand in my project without interviewing my parents...

Interview commenced at 20:00, Thursday 8th May

"So, Dad, your family is a bit interesting, isn't it?"

"Are you talking about Gramps? I'm not sure I'd go so far as to call him 'interesting'. Unusual, opinionated, embarrassing..."

"Not Gramps. I mean, well, you've been married twice."

"That's pretty common these days, you know."

"Yeah, but not everyone has one lot of children and then has children using a donor who are the same age as his grandchildren."

"Ah, that part. Yes, that is interesting, I suppose."

"Why did you bother?"

"Bother with what?"

"You know, having me and Jemima. You'd already got two children and a stepson. Why have more, especially when it was so complicated?"

"It didn't seem complicated at the time, Archie. I loved your mum and when two people love each other, quite often they want to have a family together. I love Michael and Jazz just the same, of course, but life wouldn't have been complete without you and Jemima. It's just the way it is."

"Was it hard making the decision to use donors?"

"It was a bit. I felt stupid for not being able to have children with your mum. If I hadn't, erm, done what I'd done after I'd had Jazz and Michael, I might have been able to have more children. And I'd have liked that. I can't lie to you. I did worry a bit about how you might

turn out and whether I'd look at you and think that you weren't mine, but from the moment you were born, I fell in love."

"Dad. Don't get all soppy on me."

"It's true. I've never stopped loving you, not even for a minute. And, most of the time, it never crosses my mind that you're donor conceived. You're as much my kids as the other two, more if anything, because your mum is the love of my life and our family means the world to me."

"Stop it!"

"I mean it."

"So what about our donors. Would it bother you if Jemima and I wanted to try and find them?"

"Do you want to?"

"I don't know. It's hypothetical. I'm just asking the question."

"Well, hypothetically, whatever you and Jemima want is OK by me. And, when the time comes, if you need help, I'll help you. It would be completely normal for you to wonder about your genetic roots."

"Do you think?"

"Of course. It's something that's different about you."

"I'm not sure I want to be different though."

"We're all different in one way or another, Archie. This is just your particular kind of different. Look at Hamid. He's different to most of the kids in your class. All the great thinkers and scientists and artists felt different, I'll bet. The struggle to fit in and yet to be independent is what makes us human."

"OK, you're getting a bit deep now, Dad."

"Shall I stop and say something silly?"

"Yes."

"Bottom."

"That is pretty silly."

"Yay! I've still got it."

Interview terminated at 20:14 due to Dad dancing around the room.

FRIDAY 9TH MAY

Today was supposed to be the last day of the Family Detectives project. But that was before my blabbermouth sister went and told Mrs Smithers about the conference.

Mrs Smithers now thinks me and Jemima might want to do some more work after half term!!! Well Jemima is welcome to do a hundred more interviews at the conference for all I care, but I handed my folder in. It felt a bit weird after all this time. I'm happy it's finished, but I felt quite proud of it in the end.

MY FAMILY FOLDER

At break Hamid admitted the project has made him want to visit Pakistan so he can meet his relatives. He also pointed out that one good thing has definitely come out of it - Mark Doyle seems to have backed off. It's true. Doyle hasn't tripped Ham up or called me a freak or a nerd once since that lesson where we talked about IVF.

When school breaks up Mrs Smithers always gives awards out for good work and stuff. Today she had some special awards to hand out for people who had done extra well with the project.

Jemima jumped up before her name had even been called and when we got our 'School Star' certificates she looked as if she'd just won an OSCAR.

Mrs Smithers said we should both be really proud for sharing something so special and personal with the class.

Jemima grinned and I did my tomato impression again. Genes, hey. They have a lot to answer for.

Today was the first day of the half term holidays, so Mum let me and Jemima go back over to see Cameron and we went to Mr Marsden's shop. Well, actually, she forced us to go over to see Mr Marsden. And before that she forced me to empty my money box and go with her to the garden centre to buy him a plant as an apology - because nothing says 'sorry for calling you a vampire/murderer' like a bay tree, right?

Mum dropped me, Jemima and Cam off at the shop. Then she went off to do some work in a café with her laptop. I felt like a bit of an idiot carrying a huge tree into the shop, but Mr Marsden actually looked really pleased when he saw me. Or rather, when he saw it. He probably couldn't see me behind all those leaves. I saw him though. He was peeling an orange with a very sharp-looking fruit knife and, even though I knew that he was just an ordinary old man peeling an orange, my heart started racing because he still slightly resembles a vampire and I've kind of got used to thinking he might be about to skin me alive. When he turned round at the sound of the door opening, I actually found myself jumping behind Cameron.

Mr Marsden popped an orange segment into his mouth and walked out from behind the counter. He took the plant from me and started trying it out in different places around the shop without saying anything. Eventually, he put it by the till. I was tempted to turn and go then, but I decided I'd better at least say sorry first. So I did.

"Hmmm," he nodded, seriously. "So, what've you boys been up to? Caught any more murderers?" And then he started laughing to himself, like he'd just made the funniest joke.

Ha Ha Ha Ha Ha Ha Ha
Ha Ha Ha Ha Ha Ha Ha

Next he did what we've seen him do so many times. He turned the sign on the door to 'Closed' and took us into the storeroom. I know it's silly, but I still felt a bit nervous. There's just something spooky about him with all the black he wears. I got ready to do the sweeping and tin-sorting and tidying and all the other chores I knew he was bound to give us, but instead he told us to sit down and said, "Fascinating things, families."

The diagram and the string was still up on the wall and, now I looked at it, I could see that the pictures were old black and white photos of people and the dates were of births, deaths and marriages. It was almost like the map at school, or the family tree I'd tried to draw at the beginning of the project.

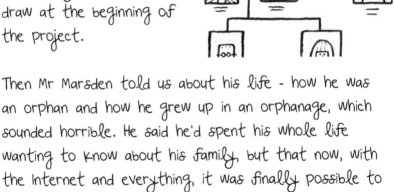

Then Mr Marsden told us about his life - how he was an orphan and how he grew up in an orphanage, which sounded horrible. He said he'd spent his whole life wanting to know about his family, but that now, with the Internet and everything, it was finally possible to trace his roots.

He showed us a picture of a guy called Frank Marsden who was born in Hathersage and who was the right age to be his dad. He was born in 1922 and died in 1972, before me and Cam were even born. Then he showed us how Frank had been married to Angela and had three kids in Liverpool, which had made him think that Frank couldn't be his dad.

But then he'd discovered that Frank Marsden had had a girlfriend called Margaret Openshaw in Hathersage in 1939. We've just done about the Second World War at school so we knew that date was the beginning of the war. What we didn't know, until he showed us, was that 1939 was also the year that Mr Marsden was born.

So, Mr Marsden reckons that Frank Marsden got this woman called Margaret pregnant and then had to go off to war. By the time it ended she must have moved house or married someone else and she'd put baby George Marsden into the orphanage in Matlock where he grew up. Meanwhile Frank must have met his wife Angela and gone off to Liverpool and had his children Harry, Trevor and Bill.

We asked what happened to Margaret. Mr Marsden said that was the million dollar question and that we were going to help him find the answer.

detective
Marsden

So we're going to do some more detective work. Much more fun than tidying up a messy stock room! Mr Marsden thinks Margaret's probably dead by now, but that we might be able to help him find some half-brothers and sisters and the thought of that obviously makes him really happy because he grew up without any family which must be really sad.

Anyway, we didn't find out any more about Margaret today, but we did talk a lot. Mr Marsden (who wants us to call him George) told us that he didn't blame his mum for putting him in an orphanage, because in those days it wouldn't have been OK for a woman to have a baby on her own and that she would have been forced to give him up.

After he told us so much about himself, I felt like he should know something about me, so I told him about my family and how Mum had had Ryan on her own until she met Dad and how now Ryan is mine and Jemima's half brother. Jemima made a face - she was in a mood with Ryan cause he used up all the milk at breakfast.

But George said, "Tough start for the lad," and "I'd have loved an older brother." That made me think about how poor Ryan never gets to see Hippy John and how, when we go on holiday me and him have this game where we see who can swim out to the buoy fastest. Ryan always lets me win, even though he's actually a way better swimmer than me - which I guess is pretty cool.

Then Cam said about how his mum had him on her own too and George called Hazel, "a reet strong lass," and surprised us by saying how great it is that women can have babies on their own these days. He said they are right to do that because all kids need is someone who loves them. And he said how much our parents must have loved us to go through all they went through with donor conception. He said that when he was growing up in the orphanage all he wanted was someone to love him. He wouldn't have cared if they were genetically connected to him or not.

"You must be the most loved kids in the world," he said.

He started going on about how our parents were so kind to think about taking us to the conference in London and letting us stay in a hotel. (Obviously he and Mum had a REALLY long phone conversation the other night!)

And he told us that he'd only been to London once. I can't believe that. I've already been three times and I'm only eleven. He couldn't believe we'd been thinking about NOT going. He said it would be fascinating to meet so many people like us and to hear their stories. "Everyone has a story to tell," he said, "you just have to look for it."

ME IN LONDON

And George is right. People aren't always what they seem. Until we did this project, I thought I knew all about the people in my class, but I didn't know about Mark Doyle's IVF and I didn't even know who Hamid lived with. And we thought Mr Marsden was a murderer, but it turns out he's just a lonely old man looking for his family. Maybe the Family Detectives project hasn't been such a bad thing after all and maybe the conference will be the same. And, if not, at least we'll get to go to the Science Museum...

LONDON HERE WE COME!

SUNDAY 25TH MAY

I'm writing this on the train home. My family are all sitting at one table and Cameron and Hazel are across the aisle. Cam's fast asleep snuggled up next to Hazel who's reading a magazine and doesn't seem to mind that Cam's drooling on her shoulder. Ryan has been to the buffet car for like, the fourth time in an hour, and is busy scoffing the soggiest looking sandwich in the

eating

drooling

zzz

history of the world. Mum, Dad and Jemima are all asleep too. It's been a pretty tiring weekend.

At least the train home is more peaceful than the one on the way to London yesterday. Poppy Braithwaite was on the next seat and she just talked and talked and talked. It was a good job Cam and me had the headphones on the iPad and could block her out and watch a film.

The conference was surprisingly OK. Actually it was pretty interesting. It was a massive room with loads of chairs and I thought half of them would be empty, but it was full up. Jemima went straight to the front of course, so that she could record everything with Dad's camera. Cameron and I sat at the back doodling on our programmes. Like this:

The title of the conference was 'Talking with Friends and Family.' In the morning there was a panel discussion with some teenagers talking about how you explain that you're donor conceived to people. A woman called Julia (who ran our afternoon workshop) asked the kids some questions and then the audience could ask questions too. There was a guy called Jack Sefton up there who looked like Harry Styles and absolutely loved himself - Jemima was following him around all day. There were four other teenagers, one was called Keira and she had cool blue streaks in her hair.

I wasn't planning on paying much attention, but I did listen to some of it, especially when they said stuff about how they'd struggled at school or with the idea of where they came from. Mostly though, we were counting how many times Jack Sefton ran his fingers through his hair (24) and how many times he said 'like' (36). Jack Sefton is what Ryan would call 'a complete twonk.'

Like...
I'm Jack Sefton,
Like...

I thought Keira was the best. Someone in the audience asked if she thought parents should be more open about donor conception. She said she thought it was good that her mum had told her from the beginning but she also said it didn't matter if parents left it until later. She had a way of making it all sound OK. She was really funny too. So even when she was talking about some tricky stuff at the end she was laughing and the audience were laughing as well.

Julia asked people about whether they would try to find out about their donors and their half-siblings when they were older. Some of them thought they would, but Keira said what I was just thinking, that she had enough people in her life without looking up random strangers and that she'd rather choose the people she hung out with because she liked them rather than hang out with people just because they shared her DNA.

Sitting there listening, I felt completely, I dunno, 'normal'? Mum and Dad always say there's no such thing as normal, so perhaps that's not the best way to describe it. I just felt like everyone there really understood me and where I was coming from.

I was a bit worried after lunch though, when it was time for the workshop, cause of standing up and talking in front of people - I've had enough of that at school to last me a lifetime. But actually we just did some games to introduce ourselves. There were all sorts of kids there. Some from solo mum families, like Cam, some in lesbian families and some with a mum and dad, like me and Jemima. It was really reassuring knowing that there are so many other kids like us out there.

Some of the younger kids had identifiable donors, but some had been conceived abroad and had anonymous donors like us. I didn't say much, but it was good to listen. I really liked this girl called Amy from London who was a double donation kid from overseas - anonymous donor like us, in a solo mum family. She was really into science, too. She wants to be a microbiologist! we swapped email addresses.

AMY

from LONDON

So at the workshop we sat round some tables and

thought about how we were different from our parents and how we are alike.

This is what I wrote...

DIFFERENCES

o My parents like garden centres. I don't.
o I like gaming until my eyes go blurry. They don't.
o They like talking about feelings. I don't.

SIMILARITIES

o Mum and me both get really annoyed with Dad singing all the time and playing his jazz music.
o Me and Mum both like jam and cream cheese sandwiches, which Dad and Jemima think are disgusting.
o We laugh at the same things.
o Dad and me look a bit alike - he's got blue eyes and used to be blonde and skinny (before he went grey and chubby.)
o We both like watching Doctor who.
o Dad and me love doughnuts and science.

So, even though we don't share the same genes, maybe I do take after my parents a bit. There are lots of ways I'm different from my family and when

I think about it, I'm quite happy about that. If I'd been genetically related to Dad, I might have inherited those fat hairy toes that he has and his sticky-out ears. And I don't know whether there's a dancing gene, but if there is, I'm soooooo glad I haven't got that from Dad. I saw him dancing something called the 'hand jive' at Jazz's wedding and it was the most embarrassing thing ever.

After the conference we met up with Ryan, who was in a really good mood because Mum let him spend the day shopping on his own in Oxford Street. He bought some amazing trainers! He says I can have them after him, if my 'puny little body ever grows'.

RYAN'S FLASH TRAINERS

This morning we had breakfast in the hotel - which was brilliant because you could just keep going up for more sausages and bacon. I had six before Mum clocked on. Then the whole family and Cam and Hazel went to the Science Museum. My favourite part (aside from the shop) was this giant space exhibition. I loved standing there looking up into the darkness at all the stars.

When I was really little I wanted to be an astronaut and I used to ask Dad whether I could be one when I grew up. He always used to say, "Someone's got to do it, Son. Why shouldn't it be you?"

Maybe I could be an astronaut-detective-forensic scientist. Or, how about...

ARCHIE NOLAN
SPACE DETECTIVE

By the time I'm working, space travel will be more common and there are bound to be new things to investigate when there is inter-planetary crime.

There was also an exhibition about genes and where we all come from. There was this quiz where you could guess which things about people were genetic and which things weren't. I was surprised that most things weren't actually passed on genetically at all. Most importantly, it turned out that the whole tongue-rolling thing is a myth. Apparently it's not genetic after all. Which explains why I have such superior skills to Jemima in that department.

There was some stuff about how the human race evolved, too. Apparently, human life began in Africa, which means that the first humans were black. And, guess what? Mrs Smithers' thing about six degrees of separation came into it too, but this time it was a bit different. Apparently, if you go back six generations, somehow or other we're all genetically related. So Mum was right and Mrs Smithers was right, too. We are <u>really</u> all connected.

So, where does all of that leave me?

Genetically I'm descended from black Africans who probably moved to Scandinavia a few thousand years ago and my donor father and mother were both tall and blonde. They might be a yachtsman and a film star or they might be a cleaner and a gardener. I might never know or maybe I will find out one day. I have the same sense of humour as my mum and like the same books as my dad, but in some ways, the people I have most in common with are a British Muslim called Hamid whose

family come from Pakistan and a donor conceived boy called Cameron whose genes are half-Hispanic.

Earlier on I was sitting with Mum, Dad, Jemima and Ryan sharing a bag of doughnuts and arguing again about which flavours are the best and I just felt really grateful for my family all of a sudden. I gave Mum a hug to thank her for taking us to London and she called me "one in a million."

That made me think. We're all one in a million, or one in seven billion to be precise. I might not know my genetic parents, but I know enough about where I come from. I also know where I am right now, with the people I love who love me too, even if Dad's glasses are falling off his nose and Jemima has her mouth wide open, snoring.

I didn't have any choice about where I came from, but where I go next is up to me. And I'm going to make it somewhere really great. Someone has to make it into space and Dad's right - why shouldn't it be me?

USE THESE PAGES TO BE YOUR OWN FAMILY DETECTIVE...

Who are the people in your family?

Write the names of other people (or pets)
who are important to you...

How are you similar to your family members?

How are you different from them?

Which five words or sentences sum up what family means to you?

Get creative with some doodle-tastic artwork.
(You could draw your friends, family or even
a character from the book!)

GLOSSARY

Anonymous donor
Donor to whom a donor conceived child or their parents has no right to identifying information. Some non-identifying information may be available.

DNA
Material that carries all the information about how a living thing will look and function. It is found in every cell of the human body. DNA is short for deoxyribonucleic acid.

Donor
Someone who voluntarily gives a part of themselves (such as sperm, eggs, an embryo, blood, an organ) for use by another person.

Donor conceived
Created with the help of eggs, sperm or embryos from a donor or donors.

Donor conception
The act of creating a baby using donated sperm, eggs or embryos.

Egg
The female reproductive cell in humans. Also known as an ovum it combines with a man's sperm in reproduction.

Egg donor

A woman who donates her eggs in order to help a person or couple conceive a baby.

Embryo

A collection of cells developed from a fertilised egg, in the early phase of development towards becoming a foetus.

Fertilisation

The union (coming together) of a human egg and sperm to produce a zygote – a fertilised egg.

Foetus

The unborn young of a human from the end of the eighth week after fertilisation to the moment of birth.

Gay

Another word to describe someone who is a homosexual (see definition on page 170.)

Gene

A particular section or portion of a cell's DNA. Genes are coded instructions for making everything the body needs, especially proteins.

Identifiable Donor

A donor who is anonymous to the parents, but is willing to be known to any children he or she has helped create from their eighteeth birthday, if they choose to have this information.

IVF

IVF stands for In Vitro fertilisation. It is the process used to create an embryo (and potential foetus) outside the body. A woman's eggs and a man's sperm are placed together in a plastic dish for fertilisation. The fertilised egg or eggs (now an embryo or embryos) are then placed in a woman's uterus (womb) in the hope a successful pregnancy will follow.

Heterosexual

Sexually attracted to people of the opposite sex. A heterosexual couple would therefore involve a woman and a man.

Homosexual

Sexually attracted to people of your own sex. For example, a homosexual couple would involve two women or two men, rather than one woman and one man.

Known donors

Donors whose identity is known at the time of donation. They may be a friend or family member and may donate at a licensed clinic or privately, outside the licensed clinic system.

Lesbian

A homosexual woman. (A woman who is sexually attracted to other women.) A lesbian couple therefore involves two women.

Sperm

Cells produced by the human male's sexual organs and released in a fluid called semen. Sperm combine with the female's egg in reproduction.

Sperm donor

A man who donates his sperm in order to help a person or couple conceive a baby.

Twins – Fraternal

Two babies born from the same pregnancy who developed from two separate eggs fertilised by two separate sperm cells. Have non-identical genetic codes. Usually, but not always, of different genders.

Twins – Identical

Two babies born from the same pregnancy who developed from a single fertilised egg that split, creating two embryos. Share an almost identical genetic code. Always the same gender.

Vasectomy

A surgical procedure for men, which is a method of birth control – meaning they can no longer be a biological parent.

DONOR
CONCEPTION
NETWORK

The publisher of this book is an organisation
called the Donor Conception Network (or DC Network).
We are based in the United Kingdom and help families who
have used donor conception. We do all sorts of things
including writing books. You may have read one of the
"Our Story" books when you were younger.

We know how important it can be to meet people in a
similar situation, people who really understand, so one of
our aims is to put parents in touch with each other. We also
like to put kids in touch with each other. Like some of the
characters in the book, some donor conceived children may
have never met another person conceived like them.
So we run events where children can meet too; picnics,
conferences and our children's workshops.

The conference Archie, Jemima and Cameron come
to in the book is based on one of our conferences and
the workshop they attend is based on our children's
workshop for donor conceived children and their
brothers and sisters aged eight to twelve years.

Ask your parents to contact us if you are
interested in finding out more.

For more information visit our website
www.dcnetwork.org or email us at enquiries@dcnetwork.org.

You can also telephone us at +44 (0)20 7278 2608.

The Nuffield Foundation is an endowed charitable trust
that aims to improve social well-being in the widest sense.
It funds research and innovation in education and social policy
and also works to build capacity in education, science and social
science research. The Nuffield Foundation has funded this
project, but the views expressed are those of the authors
and not necessarily those of the Foundation.

More information is available at www.nuffieldfoundation.org

Acknowledgements

DC Network publishes a range of books for young children up to around seven years to help explain how they came to be, but we have long known we needed something for older children. Exactly what we needed we weren't sure. We applied for a grant from the Nuffield Foundation to fund this project and we are very grateful to them for their support.

Once we had the funding to produce something our first thought was – well what do we really need? So we decided to ask the people who would know. We held a workshop for parents and their donor conceived children to talk about the project and give us direction. We talked about what sort of 'thing' we should produce, the style, the content, the format, what was important to them, what it should cover and what it shouldn't cover. The creativity and enthusiasm of that group was absolutely wonderful and they definitely steered us onto the right path. The book is for them, of course, so we just hope we've done a decent job and they approve.

We would also like to thank the British Association of Adoption and Fostering for their initial words of wisdom and Progress Educational Trust for their excellent and speedy fact-checking.

And finally, this project would not have come to fruition without the enthusiasm and commitment of DC Network Director Nina Barnsley. She took the project on with the barest brief ("produce a resource for eight to twelve-year-olds") and has crafted and guided it from the grant application right through to this wonderful finished product. She put together a great team combining Beverley's wonderful writing skills, Spike's hilarious illustrations and Andy's slick design. She also found Steph who has done an amazing job editing and project managing. This was uncharted territory for the Network; we had never produced a work of fiction before and Nina's creative skills and determination were essential to its success.